Stay Connected with Us!

Text **LOCKDOWN** to 22828 to stay up-to-date with new releases, sneak peaks, contests and more…

Like our page on Facebook:
Lock Down Publications

Join Lock Down Publications/The New Era Reading Group

Visit our website:
www.lockdownpublications.com

Follow us on Instagram:
Lock Down Publications

Email Us: We want to hear from you!

I0564748

Prologue

Dick-Whipped Damsel in Distress

"This is a really nice place you got here," Stanford Wright said, his spry gray eyes roaming the high ceiling and the multi-tiered crystal chandelier that hung from the center of it. "Reminds me of the bachelorette party I performed at back in November of last year, around the time that eighty-year-old man was trying to murder your ex." He paused to laugh while tonguing a resistant bit of steak from between his teeth. "Some rich white chick was marrying the rich black African banker, nigga from Cameroon somewhere. The girl's sister had me and one of my boys show up to this big mansion in the Hamptons. Shit was wild."

"I bet it was," Princess Kelly said, and nothing more, though her accusatory tone spoke volumes to the musclebound man sitting across the table from her.

His given name was Stanford, but that was a name only his parents and grandparents used. To everyone else he was Zoodie, an exotic dancer of some renown from Miami's infamous Little Haiti neighborhood. Prinny's close friend Aqua had hired him to entertain them during Prinny's twenty-first birthday, when they'd partied at a Palm Island mansion that had cost them $8,000 per night, and at the end of that jubilant night Zoodie had wrapped Princess's legs around his waist and carried her into the master bedroom suite.

Lock Down Publications and Ca$h
Presents

THE REAL BADDIES OF CHI-RAQ 3
SEASON 3

Written By
KING RIO

First Edition 2025

Printed in the United States of America

This is a work of fiction. Names, characters, places, and incidents either
are products of the author's imagination or are used fictitiously. Any
similarity to actual events or locales or persons, living or dead, is
entirely coincidental.

Lock Down Publications
P.O. Box 944
Stockbridge, GA 30281
www.lockdownpublications.com

Like our page on Facebook: Lock Down Publications
www.facebook.com/lockdownpublications.ldp

Just thinking of the things that took place in that king-size bed sent a chill down Princess's spine and raised goosebumps on the exposed flesh of her arms.

Standing at six feet five inches tall and weighing in at two hundred seventy-five pounds, Zoodie was built like a WWE wrestler; all muscle, zero percent body fat. His dreadlocks were clean, black, and well groomed, tied in loose knot at the back of his head. His skin was dark brown like the shell of a pecan, his teeth perfectly white like his form-fitting sweatshirt. He had clean fingernails, just an inch or so in length and manicured to perfection. Like his dreads, his eyebrows, mustache, and goatee were professionally groomed, and the cologne he wore was Calvin Klein's latest fragrance; this Princess knew because she'd purchased the same cologne for Millionaire Markio, the ex-lover she'd caught with her half-sister planted on his lap.

Kamari White was the treacherous sibling's name.

"I hate that fuckin' cologne," Prinny said matter-of-factly.

Zoodie's head jerked back; his knot of dreads bounces to and fro at the back of his head. "Damn." He furrowed his brow. "Where that come from? It's Valentine's Day, I done got all dressed up to come see you, from waaaay down in South Florida, and this is the thanks I get? You shooting down my favorite cologne?"

"It's not you," Prinny explained. She put on a smirk that felt as tight as an extra small shirt on an extra large man. "It's … never mind. You're fine I'm sorry about that."

Zoodie smiled so widely that Princess could see most of his teeth. He had a handsome, full-lipped smile. In the exotic dancing business, image was everything, and Zoodie's image was the picture of perfection. His eyes were a cool gray and had the mien of masculine kindness. His disposition was smooth and sophisticated. He was far from the usual street gang member Princess was used to dating, and perhaps that was a good thing. Perhaps he was the kind of man she needed.

"You're something," he said, and forked the last chunk of medium rare steak in his mouth. "I watch you all the time, you know. On that show. All the girls in Miami watch it. You should do a *Real Baddies of Miami.*"

"I was thinking about it." Prinny picked up her whisky glass and sipped. She had taken the liberty of eating her lunch before Zoodie's arrival. She brushed her teeth, freshened up, and put on her sexy red Prada dress over red slingback Louboutin pumps. Her Fenty lipstick was blood red, and her hair was colored blond, an homage to her musical goddess and savior, Mrs. Beyonce Knowles-Carter.

In all actuality, Princess Kelly was doing a lot more than just *thinking* about expanding her hit reality TV shows into other cities. *The Real Baddies of St. Louis* was already in production, and she was acquiring filming licenses in both Detroit and Indianapolis.

If there was nothing she learned from her primary role as producer, her secondary role as executive producer, and her tertiary role as a cast member on *The Real Baddies of Chicago*, it was that there was no such thing as too much money.

"It's crazy that you reached out to me when you did," Zoodie said, chewing. "I was just telling one of my boys about how I met you on the night of your twenty-first birthday, and how I fucked your brains out that whole night. The niggas didn't believe me for shit. Thought I was cappin'. I had to go through your girl Aqua's Instagram videos and find the ones of us at the waterfront mansion."

"Ugh. Snitching is so attractive."

"Damn, I'm a snitch now?"

Prinny's mouth spread into a wan smile that still didn't quite fit. She'd flown Zoodie in from his hometown to be with her in hopes that his presence would lift her spirits, and yet she was still in the dumps, as pensive and somber as she'd been before his arrival.

Tears burgeoned along her lower eyelids, blurring her vision. She blinked and the tears rolled down her cheeks, alerting Zoodie to her emotional distress.

His expression flashed from thoroughly smitten to sincerely empathetic, and he rose from his chair in an instant, rounding the corner of the eighteen seat dining table, a giant on a mission. He took her by the wrist, his huge, veiny hand completely encircling her Apple watch, and pulled her to her feet. The six inches her shoes added to her height allowed Prinny to rest her crying face against the unyielding boulder of one enormous pectoral muscle. Zoodie's arms were big and powerful, but they closed around her in the most delicate way.

"What's wrong? Talk to me, I talk back," Zoodie said. He rubbed her lower back, holding her close.

"It's *Valentine's* Day!" Prinny cried, as if that explained it.

Zoodie had no response to that. His warm embrace sufficed.

"My half-sister stole my man and *moved in* with him for *two whole months!* And then, when the nigga put her out last month, the bitch called *me*. Can you believe that shit? Like I would have some advice for her or something. I hung up on that ho so fast I almost broke a nail."

Zoodie chuckled. "That's funny as hell."

"It ain't *fuckin'* funny," Prinny said bitterly, as she reared back and punched the bulging rock of chest muscle she'd been resting her head against. She hurt her knuckles. "Ouch. What the hell? You on steroids or something?"

"Weights, lil baby. No 'roids, all weights." His hands moved down her back and onto the vast swells of her ass. "And just to let you know," he added, squeezing and caressing, "that lil jit I told about you is a fifteen-year-old kid from a bad neighborhood, a bad school district, and an even worse household. I took him under my wing. Got him and his fourteen=year-old brother moved in with me, and

7

I'm paying out of pocket for their 'mom's drug rehab. The jit I told about us, he's in love with you. You should see the way his eyes light up when he sees you on TV. He's the only person I've ever told about me and you. I ain't no rat."

"Shut up." Prinny wiped the tears from her face, titling her head back to stare up at her black Hercules. "No, but seriously. I salute you for taking those boys in. That's some real shit. I saw them on your page, but I thought they were your nephews."

"Nope. Complete strangers. They tried to rob me one night in Overtown. Caught me getting out of my Porsche in a liquor store parking lot, and Tayren – the one that like you – he pulled a pistol on me. This was two years ago, when Tayren was thirteen and Tory was just a scrawny little twelve-year-old. Now he's the bigger one."

"What happened with the gun?" The thrilling story had torn Prinny right out of her sad and dismayed theater of the mind. Now she was in that liquor store parking lot, watching the two pubescent thugs accost Zoodie and demand his money. "Finish the story. Did you punch him and take the gun? Did you talk him into putting it down and letting you go?"

"Neither," Zoodie said with an animated chuckle. "I was reaching in my pocket for the cash when Tayren shot me. Hit me right here." He slipped one arm from around Prinny's waist and patted the outside of his left thigh. His gray jeans were stonewashed. His shoes were Celine Homme, like his sweatshirt. "Didn't do more than crease me, really, but I felt the sting and that scared the piss outta me. So I took off running. Tayren shot at me as I ran. Then he and Tory went joy riding in my truck. I'm the only one out of my four brothers that didn't fall into the streets. We have a group chat, and after I texted them about what went down, it didn't take long for them to track down the kids who'd done it. By the time I left the hospital my brothers had them tied up in this abandoned house, scarred half to death."

"Oh my Jesus."

"They were fine," Zoodie assured her. "I cut them loose myself. Took them home and tried to have a talk with Tiny, their mother, but she was too high to comprehend any of my words. Plus, their refrigerator was even emptier than their kitchen cabinets, their clothes were filthy, and their beds weren't beds at all, just three or four blankets on their bedroom floor. So I took them back home with me."

"As you should have. God gon' bless you for that."

"He already did," Zoodie said, taking Prinny's face in his hands and lowering his lips onto hers.

Zoodie had the world's greatest kisses. His tongue darted into her mouth, and she tasted the vestiges of his meal. Steak sauce. Cheddar cheese from the macaroni, butter and seasoning from his baked potato. His lips felt softer than her own skin.

When she finally pulled back she saw that she'd gotten a significant amount of her cosmetics — lipstick, eye shadow, foundation, et cetera — on his two thousand dollar sweatshirt. She opened her mouth to apologize, but then Zoodie went to his knees, shoved her dress up to her waist, and began kissing and licking at the smoothly shaven nexus of her thighs.

She forgot all about the apology.

"You smell so good down here," Zoodie proclaimed, "I could bottle it up and sell it."

Princess snickered and then gasped, because one second Zoodie was lifting her right leg onto his left shoulder and the next second he stood straight up, raising her high in the air while at the same time sliding the flat of his tongue along the rigid nub of her clitoris.

Although she was quite certain that he wouldn't let her fall, Prinny still took hold of his dreads— just to be on the safe side. He shouldered her other leg and continued the course. Sucking. Licking. Kissing. Blowing. She rotated her hips, grinding against his mouth, her eyelashes fluttering blissfully.

It didn't take him long to get her there. Three and a half minutes, maybe even four. When the orgasms hit her she made a sound that was partly a moan and partly the scream of a banshee on crystal meth.

Zoodie said, "Yeeeaah. Give me that juice." Emphatically enunciating each work, his big hands holding her just under her rib cage. "This is what I daydreamed about on the flight here. It's the one thing I remember most about that night we spent together: how wet you get when you come."

Prinny was still seeing stars, so she offered no reply. She was hardly even aware of Zoodie lowering her onto the mahogany dining table. What brought her back to reality was the sight of Zoodie's chest as he peeled off his makeup-smeared sweat-shirt and the white t-shirt he wore underneath it. Not just his chest but his abs too. And his arms. And his shoulders.

Unable to endure the wait, Prinny reached forward between her parted legs and undid his belt for him. Zoodie did the rest, first kicking off his shoes, and then removing his jeans and underwear and placing them on the seat of the chair. From the pocket of his jeans he retrieved a Magnum condom; this also went barely noticed by Prinny', for her eyes were transfixed on Zoodie's huge black dick.

Famed for both its incredible length and inconceivable girth, Zoodie the Stripper's dick was a prodigious python of a penis. The kind of dick that should be required to come with a glaring red *WARNING* sign. The kind of dick that had likely dislocated a jaw or two. The kind of dick that needed its own name and social security number.

Prinny had an inch or so of cognac left in her whiskey glass. She picked it up and downed it in a single swallow as Zoodie's sheathed his formidable member in rubber and stepped forward. Muscles upon muscles rippled beneath his skin. The VVS diamonds in his two plain tennis chains glistened around his neck, as did the ice in his Audemars Piguet wristwatch.

"Tayren asked me if I could ever see myself getting married," he said. "I told him it would have to be to you or Porsha Williams. A special kinda thick, you know? Your body is perfect. Take off that dress. I wanna see all of this."

Prinny was removing her dress and thinking that if there was anyone worthy of breaking her three months of celibacy it was Zoodie — especially after hearing the heroic tale of how 'he'd rescued those two young boys from the slums even after they'd held him at gunpoint, shot him, shot *at* him, and stolen his Porsche — when the feel of his fat cockhead breaching her slippery nether lips ripped her right out of that reverie.

Her brow creased and her jaw slackened. She filled her lungs with air and held it in until he got the first couple of inches inside her. Then, exhaling shakily, she gripped the edge of the table and held on.

Zoodie's penetrative thrusts were slow and deep. He folded her legs back, sucked on her perky breast, kissed her in the mouth. He said things like "Damn, you got some good-ass pussy." and "Look at all that cream on my dick." and "You gon' make me nut." And Prinny couldn't deny that if felt *great* having a dick so long and thick stretching her wide and deep.

But there was something missing.

She knew what it was, knew *exactly* what it was, but she didn't want to think about it, so she shoved it to the back of her mind and enjoyed the ride.

Zoodie fucked her good for the next seven or eight minutes. Halfway through, fiddling with her distended clitoris, Prinny came again, an orgasm that proved to be even more powerful than the first. This time the scream that accompanied her moan was like a banshee with a bullhorn. Her climatic cream dribbled down over her sporadically contracting sphincter and dripped onto the table beneath her,

Three or four minutes after that Zoodie freed his lengthy tool from her stretched and battered hole, snatched off his condom, and stroked forth half a dozen stripes of ejaculate, one of which reached way up into the hollow of her throat. The stuff was thick, white, and sticky. Like frosting on a honey bun.

"Ssshhit," Zoodie said. The sibilant word was followed by a spastic shiver. Even his lower lip tremble. Coaxing the last few globules of semen out of his slowly deflating appendage, Zoodie muttered a word that some might consider a curse to God, though Prinny knew he was a deeply spiritual man. "We can ... we can go... another round. Just... give me a... couple of minutes."

Prinny snickered. "Take your time, big zaddy." she said, her C-cups rising and falling as she struggled to catch her own breath. "We got all weekend."

Chapter 1

"So what's the word bitch?" Kari 'Thick Doll' Washington asked her dear friend and secret lover, Talisha 'Aqua' Mason. "I know Day-Day got some'n good planned for you. I mean, it is Valentine's Day. I saw all those roses he sent you in that IG post, but quality time trumps all that miscellaneous shit."

Aqua raised her right shoulders in a half shrug. She had something to say on the subject, but her strong and disdainful opinion was too deep and too revealing for the public to know about, and her snow-drizzled, cherry-red Rolls-Royce Cullinan was outfitted with interior cameras that recorded really good audio, so she kept her pretty lips sealed and only offered the shrug.

They were stuck at a red light on Chicago Avenue, just outside the notorious K-Town neighborhood that had spawned Karionna Patrice Washington. Like Kari, the area was cold, as gloomy as it was ominous, and hardened by the street gang warfare that had plagued the community since time immemorial. However, despite the chill and the high potential for violence, the blocks were alive with activity. Motorists came and went in either directions, some hauling bouquets of sweet-smelling flowers for their significant others, some concealing pistols with extended magazines for their significant enemies. There were some tax paying denizens heading to and from work, friends visiting friends, sons checking on mothers. Crackheads prowled the streets, both afoot and inside their rust-laden vehicles, ostensibly in search for their next narcotic escape.

The two quasi-famous reality TV stars sat in the supreme comfort of the luxury sport-utility vehicle that had cost Aqua four hundred and eighty thousand dollars – cash. Idling in the street behind them were two black Escalades, inside which sat a Minority Television Network film crew and three burly black bodyguards. In the Cullinan, Aqua and Kari both smiled demurely, knowing that their words and images were likely to be heard and seen by the forty-seven million viewers that tuned in weekly to watch *The Real Baddies of Chicago.*

"I'll tell you what I *am* looking forward to," Aqua said to change the subject. "Getting back on that pole! I can't *wait* to walk back into the locker room, change into some'n sexy, and then go out there and do my lil dance."

"I'm with you when you're right!" Kari exclaimed, her voice brimming with mirthful excitement.

The palms of their neatly manicured hands slapped together in an exhilarating high-five.

This evening, on Valentine's day of all days, the strip club where the two young women had gained all their fame and glory was having a so-called Grand Reopening, an event so monumental that it had made it to the front page of *The Chicago Sun-Times...* though not necessarily for the brightest of reasons.

Three months ago, on a cool and dreary Friday afternoon not unlike the one Aqua and Kari were currently experiencing at a red light in that West Side intersection, an 81-year=old Vietnam war veteran had murdered six men in the Queen of Diamonds parking lot. The old man, identified by police as Herbert T. Harris, had shot and killed a seventh man in the alleyway behind the world-renowned strip joint before he and a masked female accomplice were seen forcing a man into a dark-colored Range Rover at gunpoint and driving away, never to be seen or heard from again. The seven dead men were known to frequent the establishment alongside its sole proprietor, Roy Sullivan, a.k.a. Weezy, whos killed in a car bombing outside of Streetville's Sheraton Suites just before the Range Rover with Herbert in it went cruising out of the alley behind Queen of Diamonds, leading authorities to believe that the old man had detonated the car bomb remotely before seeming to vanish from the face of the earth.

The light turned green. Aqua flexed one high-heeled Gucci boot on the gas pedal, and her Cullinan launched forward.

"I wonder who'll be running the club now," Aqua said, eyeing the road ahead through the lightly tinted lenses of her Gucci sunglasses.

"Probably Weezy's ex-wife," Kari surmised. "I can't remember if her name is Claudia or Claudine, but I do know that her beachfront mansion out there in Malibu burned to the ground in that big California wildfire. Saw that on *The Shade Room*."

"Nahhh." Aqua wagged her yellowish-brown head from side to side. A few blond strands of hair from her obscenely expensive lace-front wig fell down over her brow and she made no move to finger them back in place. "I don't see her moving back to Chicago. Even if she does, she won't want anything to do with Queen of Diamonds. I'm thinking one of their kids. They got like four or five kids. One of Weezy's sons is a wannabe rap star."

"Weezo," Kari said.

"Yeah, that's him. Has all those YouTube videos where he's hanging out with his boys at those AirBnB mansions and swerving lane to lane in those luxury rental cars, flashing his daddy's money and talking like he's some kinda gangster. Claims he's from Englewood, but that boy was raised in *East* Chicago. That's in Indiana, not Illinois."

Aqua raised her shoulder again. "Whatever the case may be, I'm just glad the club's reopening. It's gon' be *too* lit up in that bitch tonight. You remember that night Diddy came through? When I was still on Preferred Shift? That night I brought home twenty grand. I bet we take home at least that tonight."

The notion excited Kari so much so that she exposed her tongue and did a little dance in her seat, while Aqua raised the volume on the Mello Buckzz song she'd already had playing on low.

The two young black women were both strikingly beautiful, as were all the girls Queen of Diamonds employed. Aqua was a mixed race stunner of East European and African American bloodline. Her pretty lips were pink, full, and succulent, her cheeks had dimples in them, and her doe-like eyes were hazel in color. Somewhat of a pain freak, she had piercings all over, from her tongue and left nostril to her nipples and clitoris. Her shape was the Queen of Diamonds standard: nice tits, small waist, big butt. Dancing at Chicago's premier strip club had gotten her farther than she'd ever imagined possible. Now she was a reality T.V. star with over five million Instagram followers, and NBA star finance, and a suburban mansion worth over twenty million dollars. Sure, Herman was a serial cheater, and maintaining the mortgage on her extravagant home was like climbing a mountain of marbles, but what was life without challenges?

Aqua's black fur coat was a Russian sable that stopped at her slender waist. Her black leather pants were Gucci and had cost her three grand. The canary yellow diamond on her ring finger weighed ten carats and had cost her man $2 million.

Kari was a twenty-seven-year-old of medium brown complexion and average height. Her dark brown hair — also a lace front — was bobbed and cute. Her pink-and-white Fendi sweater matched her skintight sweat pants and sneakers. Her natural mien was composed, quiet, and reserved, and it returned in a flash as Aqua spun the steering wheel onto Monticello Avenue and pulled over to park in front of a three-story brownstone that was the domicile of their least favorite castmate.

Aqua sighed and shook her head.

Kari clenched her teeth and let loose a throaty groan of pure disgruntlement.

"I swear to God," Kari said, "I cannot stand this ho."

"She means well," Aqua said in real earnest.

"Can't we just skip this segment?"

'Nope. We need to talk her out of all the petty social media drama she keeps getting herself into before somebody gets hurt."

"How can we talk her into doing anything when this crazy bitch won't stop talking long enough to listen?"

Aqua sighed again. "What can I say? She's Blabbermouth Blicky. The name says it all."

Chapter 2

Blaire Ketchum was a Puerto Rican baddie with a not so Puerto Rican name. Her stage name Blicky Nicky, had been with her for years, namely because she'd grown up listening to Nicki Minaj's music on repeat and had always considered herself among the rap queen's legions of Barbz. She'd only recently become aware that at last half of her *Real Baddies* co-stars called her Blabbermouth Blicky behind her back, and now, as she stood peering out her living room window with her own two cameramen behind her, watching as Aqua pulled over behind her boyfriend's triple black Dodge Challenger Hellcat and parked, Blicky sucked a tooth and rolled her eyes and sneered.

"Ol' fake ass bitches," Blicky said in the bitterest of tones. She knew the cameras were rolling and didn't care. "Hoes wanna call me *Blabbermouth*. Y'all don't even wanna go there with the nicknames, because I will go there by train, boat, or plane. This ho call herself Aqua when her pussy dry as sandpaper. And Thick Doll, yo losin' a lil bit too much weight, ho. They gon' start callin' you *Thin* Doll real soon."

She threw the curtain back in place and stomped across the pine floor to her pink leather sofa, where she flopped down, wearing a heavy pink kimono and fuzzy pink slippers. Her coffee table was a teal cube of marble with an ovoid slab of glass laid over it and a Persian rug the same oval shape as the glass laid under it.

Blicky picked up her iPhone and her vape pen from the table; she'd been standing just across the street from Weezy's

Bentley coupe when it was blown halfway to the moon with him in it, and since then she'd taken up vaping.

Sucking in a mouth full of smoke, she texted Aqua to come right in; the front door was unlocked. Then she texted Zephyra, the cousin she'd hired as a housemaid as soon as Princess Kelly cut the first *Real Baddies* paycheck, and told her to bring in the snacks and drinks she'd already prepared in the kitchen.

The two bitches came in with their own camera crew and three bodyguards in tow. Aqua and Thick Doll sat in the two overstuffed, pink leather armchairs, while their cameramen took up positions behind them.

Blicky put on a smile that was as fake as movie money. It was a good thing that Aqua and Thick Doll hadn't sat on the sofa with her. She might have slapped a ho on general principle.

"What the hell you bitches want?" Blicky asked, struggling to keep the faux smile turned on.

The sound of a sucked tooth came from Thick Doll as Aqua said, "We just came to check on you. See if you're ready for this big reopening. I know I am."

"Mmm hm," Blicky hummed dubiously.

"Look," Aqua went on." I know you're still probably upset over what happened to Weezy— we all are —but you gotta let that go. Taking out your pain on other people is not the way to—."

"Bitch, please." Blicky interjected, regarding Aqua through a dense haze of smoke. "I know why y'all came over here. You think I'm fuckin' stupid? That ho Shmoney Rose came for me on the Gram, so now it's up there with her and her weak-ass best friend Cherish Taylor. And fuck Sasha too, wit' her horse face, and that fat-ass pig nose. I see why they call that bald headed ho Sasha the Stallion; it ain't 'cause she thick it's 'cause she got a mother fuckin' *horse* head. Ol' ugly ass bitch."

Thick Doll snorted a laugh; Blicky shot her a venomous look and then turned her attention back to Aqua just as the curvy young mulatto was heaving a sigh and crossing her legs at the ankles.

"And why you takin' up for Shmoney anyway?" Blicky had been *dying* to ask Aqua the question. "Didn't you catch her fuckin' your fiancé in the backseat of her Bently truck? Now you takin' up for the bitch?"

Aqua's pretty yellow face flushed red. "That's neither here nor there."

"*Bullshit*! Bitch, that's here *and* there. I would've knocked that ho from here to *over* there."

Thick Doll mumbled, "This girl is nuts."

Blicky said, "How about you *suck* these nuts? Huh? How 'bout that? Just pop 'em right in ya mouth like—" She made a loud *pop* with her thick pink lips. "How 'bout that?"

Thick Doll pressed the tip of an index finger against the center of her forehead and laughed quietly.

"Like I thought, ho," Blicky Nicky continued. "Yeah. I know all about you. I heard all about you, *Karionna.* You shot Shayna Harwell from down there on Lockwood. Shot four or five of her cousins too, when they tried to jump you at that house party on Pulaski. Well, guess what? Guess what, *Karionna*. I shoot back, and I don't miss. My daddy was a marksman. A boxer too. And he taught me everything he knew."

That got Thick Doll's attention. She straightened her posture and stared straight at Blicky, wrinkling her forehead like a raisin. "First off, I ain't shot nobody. And second, I know you ain't threatenin' me."

"And if I was?" Blicky tilted her head to the side. "And if I was, ho? The fuck you gon' do about it? Bitch, I'm from the O Parkway Gardens. We ain't for none."

Zeffy came in with a platter of crackers and cheeses pinched between the thumb and finger of one hand. In her other hand she held a serving tray with three drinks balanced on it. She was just as pretty as Blicky, only she was more slender and lithe, and her long black hair was curly instead of straight, and her septum was pierced with a thin silver hoop.

"Henny on deck!" Zeffy said, sounding almost as overcharged as her garrulous relative.

Thick Doll snatched a snifter of cognac off the tray and drank down half its contents in a single swallow. Watching her cute round face twist up against the burn, Blicky wished she'd had the mind to piss into that particular glass. Zeffy would assuredly have been against it— a weak ass bitch, that Zephyra— but the notion brought a genuine grin to the corners of Blicky's juicy lips.

Taking her own ballooned glass in hand, Blicky Nicky turned back to Aqua.

"Shmoney Rose started this whole shit, Aqua. On Von, I ain't never said shit bad about that musty ho until she came for me. She went on that podcast and came for me in the worst fuckin' way. All Prinny said was, 'How do you feel about Blicky Nicky joining the cast?' And that raggedy, janky, stanky, funky-booty ass bitch gon' sit there and say. 'Ugh. Blabbermouth Blicky.' Like she know me or some'n. That ho don't know me like that. But don't even trip. Watch. Me and that bitch gon' get real fuckin' acquainted when we get in that locker room tonight. Ten o'clock. We got a date."

And then, inspired by a rhyme she'd heard in *The Nutty Professor*, Blicky freestyled her own little jingle:

"Friday night at *ten*… Hit that ho in the *chin*… She won't speak *again*! Hey, hey, hey, *Hey*!"

Aqua shrieked with laughter. Thick Doll fell back in her chair laughing so hard that some of her drink sloshed out over her wrist. The MTN camera crew and the bodyguards howled, with Mike the cameraman going into a coughing fit as he doubled over and clutched a forearm to his skinny gut— though he kept his rail-thin camera arm ramrod straight in the air, ever mindful of the $39.50=an-hour he made to film the girls for the show.

Blicky Nicky snickered too, albeit for a different reason. She had violence on the brain. Her neat little rhyme may have been funny, but it was far from a joke.

She and Tiara Moore, a.k.a. Shmoney Rose, had a motherfucking date, and she had plans to stomp that bitch's face through the floor as soon as she got close to do it.

Chapter 3

"YoungNya... on Fiyah... Forgiatos, gold wires
Put these bitches to rest, why? 'Cuz, I'm too up
and these hoes tired
Right hand on the Bible, Nya the truth, baby
these hoes liars
Face-to-face in the booth, I bet I wear 'em out
like old tires..."

The Mercedes-Benz G-Wagon rocked on its suspension as it four occupants— Jaresha, Tammy, Shalonda, and Noesha— bounced in their plush black leather seats, rapping along to the YoungNya song Jaresha Brady had turned up so loud that her entire SUV seemed to vibrate in sync with the throbbing bassline.

There were several reasons why the four young black women were so replete with excitement. For one, YoungNya was a fellow west-sider like the four of them (Noesha was one of her closest friends), and the feisty young rap princess had recently collected two Grammy Awards, indelible wins that had made the whole city proud. For two, the much talked about Grand Reopening of Queen of Diamonds was big news for Jaresha, the voluptuous redbone exotic dancer who performed at the strip club under the moniker Kitty Jae. And thirdly, last but *certainly* not least, the screenplay Jaresha had written for her first horror movie had been accepted by none other than MTN Films. She'd signed the deal two months ago, shortly after walking into MTN Tower with

$500,000 in a duffle bag and a look of unshakable equanimity in her eyes, but today it felt more official. Today there were casting calls taking place all across the nation for the movie she'd written. Her attorney — Jazzmine Ellis of the prestigious Bostic and Staples law firm — had emailed her just thirty minutes ago saying that Halle Berry had arrived at a table reading in New York City.

Halle Berry.

The immense joy that had set Jaresha's adrenal glands ablaze was greatly needed. She was usually an unfailingly friendly and kind woman, with a sweet temperament and a heart of gold. Her smile was invigorating. Her bluntness and honesty, though excessive, endeared her to friends. She was an avid horror fan, which explained why the left side of her shapely body, from shoulder to ankle was covered with tattoos of her favorite horror movie villains— but never in life had she imagined that an 81-year-old man, with skin as black as the night was dark, would terrify her in ways that no scary movie could ever come close to doing. The experience had frightened her into a bottomless depression that had snatched her down as swiftly and suddenly as an undertow, and it seemed like the harder she fought against it the deeper it dragged her down.

Jaresha remembered it like it was yesterday; her standing beside a ruggedly handsome, dark-hued gangster named Jahlil Owens, inside a luxury car garage that flanked the grandest mansion she'd ever seen up close. Her boyfriend, Anton Hicks, was squatting low a foot or so in front of her, engaged in a dice game with a dozen or so other men, all of them lifelong members of the infamous Traveling Vice Lords street gang. There had been other girls in the garage, some of them lingering near the big stainless steel refrigerator that had been filled with gold bottles of champagne, others admiring the Ferraris, Lamborghinis, Bugattis, and other high-priced foreign vehicles, but Jaresha "Kitty Jae" Brady had maintained her standing role as a sideline spectator of the craps game, not only to keep watch over her man but also in hopes of procuring a fling with Jahlil, he was married to Tirzah Lyon, her good friend and former hairstylist, but so what? Married men cheated on their wives more often than white cops shot black men, and Anton had stepped out on Jaresha more times than she could count on all her fingers and toes.

She'd been studying Jah out the corner of her eye when, on his smartphone, he was tagged in a Facebook video showing the horrific aftermath of a bombing that had destroyed a local barber's home on 15th Street and Trumbull Avenue, in the North Lawndale neighborhood in which both Jaresha and Jah were born and raised. She'd commented that the barber had cut her son's hair only a few days prior.

And that was when the boy named Archibald Wilson made his unsightly appearance.

Notably short and tremendously ugly, cock-eyed and fat-nosed, the boy had approached her from the side and slithered in between her and Anton. He had introduced himself as Lil Archie, smiling broadly enough to show that his teeth were spread out like a hand of playing cards, rubbing one hand forward over the waves in his hair and announcing that he had gone to Rev the barber that very same day. He'd tried to entice Jaresha by licking his lips like a reptile and spitting the little bit of game he had, and she'd brusquely shot him down. Anton had risen up behind him a moment later, the big man looming over the little man like a skyscraper over a two-story home.

But then, before Anton "Two Ton" Hicks could utter a single word of discontent, the distant crack of a gunshot had frozen everyone in place.

BOW!

From a hundred yards away.

Two Ton's huge right arm was flung behind his back. Before Jaresha had time to process that odd rearward swing— and the mist of blood that sprayed out with it— the hideous boy who'd introduced himself as Lil Archie suffered a gunshot wound to the left side of his scalp that caved in his head on that side, (momentarily straightening that cocked eye of his) and blew the entire right side of his head completely off. Bits and pieces of brain and bone had splashed into Jaresha's open mouth. She'd gasped and choked on that mass of cranial stew. That sickening memory still haunted her dreams.

Her waking hours were equally haunted. Two Ton's right arm was amputated just above the elbow and every time Jaresha looked at the bandaged stump she was reminded that she'd provided information to his shooter in exchange for that duffle bag full of new and uncirculated hundred dollar bills she'd used to secure her movie deal.

Had she not snapped and forwarded numerous photos of Weezy's brand-new Bentley coupe to Herbert Harris's cell phone, the former owner of Queen of Diamonds would be alive today.

The exchange of those pics for that $500,000 was the epitome of a necessary evil, and yet it still ate at her very soul.

So yes, she needed this moment with her girls. She needed it about as badly as Donald Trump needed to grab hold of some random woman's pussy.

"Man, cousin," Tammy said, reaching forward from the backseat to smack Jaresha on the shoulder of her black Louis Vuitton bomber jacket, "Nya tweaked *out* on this one."

"Wait, wait, wait," said Noesha Long, a.k.a New-New. The green-eyed yellowbone, famed for her angelic beauty long before she gained almost three million Instagram followers for no reason other than the fact that she and YoungNya were close friends, was perched shotgun with her iPhone in one immaculately manicured hand, pointing at something outside her window with the index finger of her other hand. "Ain't that Aqua's Cullinan? I believe it is."

Jaresha slowed her SUV as they were passing Monticello and looked out New-New's window, following the trajectory of that French-manicured forefinger. Sure enough, there was Aqua's cherry-red Rolls-Royce Cullinan, parked outside Blicky Nicky's brownstone home with two black SUVs parked behind it.

Blicky Nicky, the stunningly attractive, repulsively annoying nutcase, who'd saved Two Ton's life by tying her t-shirt around his bleeding arm after he was shot.

A *Chicago Sun-Times* news reporter had tracked Blicky down two days later. Part of the interview, as well as a photo of a broadly smiling Blicky Nicky, had made it onto the front page. Several other prominent news outlets – Time, CNN, MSNBC, Newsweek, MTN, BBC — had run stories on Blicky Nicky's heroic efforts to save the life of a fellow Chicagoan, and she'd made appearances on all the local radio and TV stations, including on *Windy City Live* with Val Warner. Applying that tourniquet had made Blaire Ketchum a hometown hero, a household name— and also the newest addition to Jaresha and Two Ton's relatively small circle of friends.

Heaving a sigh, Jaresha said, "They're probably filming. That's Blicky Nicky's house, and you know she's on *The Real Baddies of Chicago* now."

The corners of New-New's shimmery pink lips ascended an inch to form a remarkably pretty smile. "I can't even lie," she said, "that girl is the main reason everybody's so pressed to see Season Three. She is a whole fool on social media. I was already following her before she even got on the show. Did y'all see that video of her going live on Insta after Weezy's car blew up? "

"Mm-hm." Jaresha nodded her head and drove on. "She picked up one of his fingers and showed it to the camera. That girl is nuts."

Just then, Shalonda lurched forward and smacked her big sister on the shoulder.

"We should pull up over there!" Shalonda suggested in a tone pitched high with excitement. "If they're filming when we walk in we could end up on the show!"

Shalonda's complexion was brown like lightly toasted bread. Her wig was orange and styled in an asymmetrical bob. She had dense eyebrows, a patrician nose, and thin lips that were perpetually poised like a duck's lips. A thin gold chain descended from the piercing in her left earlobe to the piercing in the rear of her left nostril. Light hazel striations flecked the dark brown irises of her bloodshot eyes. Just three days past her nineteenth birthday, Shalonda was as slender and beautiful as Zoe Saldana – and as mentally unhinged as Blicky Nicky.

"Nope," Jaresha said. "You and Blicky are a bad combination. I can deal with one of y'all at a time, but I can't do both. I just can't."

The explanation, delivered with such calmness and candor, elicited a soft giggle from Tammy, who was pretty and petite like Shalonda and reddish-brown in complexion like Jaresha. She was sitting next to Shalonda, texting on her iPhone. Shalonda sucked a tooth and regarded her giggling cousin with a cold stare; if looks could kill, Tammy would have died right then and there.

Jaresha watched the one-sided staredown in the reflection of her rearview mirror, and she was glad that, just half a minute later, she was able to turn onto Kilpatrick and pull over in front of the yellow clapboard house where Shalonda's boyfriend, Colby, stood waiting on the front porch.

Shalonda's fiery scowl slackened into something a lot less severe as she looked out Tammy's window. Colby— a stocky, rodent faced boy in a plum-colored Bears hoodie and skinny jeans— was all smiles, holding a bouquet of long-stemmed red roses in one ashy-knuckled hand. The six ribbons wrapped around his other fist were attached to half a dozen Valentine's Day balloons with a variety of amorous exhortations imprinted on them. He held up his smartphone in the hand with the ribbons coiled around it, presumably recording video of his girlfriend's arrival, video that would undoubtedly be uploaded to social media within the next couple of minutes.

It was times like this that made Jaresha glad she'd opted for darkly tinted windows.

"I'll see y'all at QOD," Shalonda said, opening her door.

"Don't let that boy come with you if he's dressed like that," Jaresha said.

"For real, though," Tammy added "His whole vibe is on bum-da-dum-dum. Look like he borrowed that hoodie from Pookie off *New Jack City.*"

"Keep talkin' shit about my motherfuckin' man," Shalonda said, "and you gon' need to borrow some *teeth.*"

Tammy rolled her eyes and waved off Shalonda's threat as if it were nothing more than a bothersome fly. She went back to texting on her phone…until she heard Shalonda hawking up a mouthful of spit.

Her eyes went wide as she turned to look at her younger cousin. "Bitch, I swear to God, if you—"

Shalonda spat a copious spray of saliva into Tammy's pretty face. Instinctively, Tammy drew her lips in over her teeth and reached out to grab hold of Shalonda's hair. Failing that, she tried for the furry gray collar of Shalonda's puffy pink Moncler coat. But Shalonda was too swift, too limber. She ducked low and slipped out of the SUV with the alacrity of a frightened alley cat, throwing the door shut against the clawed hand and voicing her own triumphantly delightful little giggle as she darted around the rear of the SUV and onto the sidewalk

Having watched the entire situation play out in her rearview mirror (her eyes and mouth had gone wide with stunned amusement when the actual spitting took place), Jaresha acted quickly to keep Tammy from hopping out and embarrassing Shalonda in front of her boyfriend.

She locked the doors when Tammy reached to open hers and toed the gas pedal down far enough to launch the G-Wagon away from the curb so rapidly that the propulsion threw all its passengers back in their seats.

"Nuh-uh. Hell nah. Stop this car. That lil girl got me fucked up. Pull over, Jaresha. Pull… the fuck… over."

Tammy dug a tissue out of her red leather YSL handbag and began wiping the spittle from her face. The viscous length of slime that dangled from her left eyebrow had green snot mixed in with it. Her first attempt at wiping it away was to no avail as it peeled away from the tissue and smacked wetly onto her eyelid, effectively sealing her eye shut.

A low, feral growl crawled up to the back of Tammy's throat and stayed there a moment, like a ravenous black panther crouched in the dark recess of a cave. She tipped her head back and screamed.

"I'm beating her ASS!"

"And I ain't jumping in" Jaresha said. "She deserves that ass whoopin'. Only reason I pulled off is 'cause I know that boy would've uploaded that video to World Star as soon as the fight was over."

"I don't wanna wait, Reesh. Turn around. *Please* turn around. All you gotta do is pull up and give me *one minute* with that hoe. Sixty motherfuckin' seconds. That's all the fuck I need."

Jaresha only shook her head and focused on the slush-slick road ahead. She didn't even consider turning her truck around. Tammy was one of Jaresha's favorite cousins, but Shalonda was Jaresha's little sister; as much as she wanted to stay out of it, deep down she knew that was a true impossibility. Shalonda and Tammy had come to blows twice before, and both times Jaresha had ended up tagging herself in and beating Tammy to the ground forgetting the best of her sister.

"That was low," New-New said, and shook her head—not like a person propounding a negative; but the way a dog will shake himself after coming in from the rain. "Yuck, I cannot believe she did that. I know y'all family and all, but I would have to disown my cousin if she did somethin' like that to me."

"I'm fucking her up," Tammy stated matter-of-factly. She was already back on her phone, texting, her thumbs moving in a furious blur. Beads of spittle glistened on the shoulder of her red leather Chanel bomber jacket.

Holding the steering wheel more firmly than was necessary, Jaresha drove on to her destination. YoungNya was shooting a music video at the Visionary Lounge, a five-story nightclub that stood at the northwest corner of Chicago Avenue and Laramie, and she'd invited the three of them to be a part of it. New-New had flown in from Memphis, where her latest beau—a squat, stolid B-list actor named Donald Beatrice—lived with his wife and two children. Jaresha had picked New-New up from O'Hare airport just over an hour ago, and she'd regaled Jaresha with all the juicy details of her messy situationship as they wheeled her luggage out to the truck.

The YoungNya song had segued into Psalm One's "Plenty of Wins". Jaresha cranked the volume almost to the speaker's distortion point and breathed a gusty sigh of frustration. Earlier today, she'd found great joy in knowing that Blicky Nicky and Shmoney Rose were probably going to fight when they crossed paths at the Queens of Diamonds reopening. Now there was a second QOD fight on the schedule: Shalonda versus Tammy.

As if reading Jaresha's mind, New-New said, "I don't know how they're going to make it sitting at the same V.I.P. table at QOD tonight. That's a recipe for disaster."

"Girl, I was just thinking the same thing," Jaresha said. She glanced at her rearview mirror and saw that Tammy was still glowering at her smartphone, typing like a woman gone mad.

Two minutes later, as they were turning into the parking lot behind The Visionary Lounge, a dark gray Ford Explorer with two twentysomething-year-old black men in it came trundling in behind them. The Explorer parked in the far corner of the lot, far away from where Jaresha pulled in just behind the towering yellow edifice.

She never even noticed them.

Chapter 4

"Here goes nothing," Big Gabby said.

She drew in a deep breath and held it in her lungs as she stepped forward onto the scale. The black perforated runner felt soothing beneath her bare feet. She lowered her eyes slowly , without moving her head, as if she expected to find a rattle snake coiled in front of her chubby brown toes.

There was no serpent lying in wait, but the black digital number that flashed onto the rectangular display screen was just as alarming.

301 pounds

The breath she'd been holding in came out in a disappointed whoosh. She stood there a moment longer, staring down at that godawful number.

"Ain't this about a bitch?" she asked herself the question in a high-pitched voice.

Absurdly, she realized that she was disturbed more by that single extra pound than she was disturbed about the even three hundred. She knew she'd been gaining a lot these past three months— in the aftermath of the car bombing that killed Weezy and half a dozen of his gang-related cohorts, Big Gabby had traded in her Planet Fitness gym membership for a Netflix subscription and rekindled the secret love triangle she'd had with Hostess and Little Debbie.

The white metal frame of the scale issued a grating creak as big Gabby stepped backward on the balls of her feet. Leaving the restroom on tiptoe, she re-entered her adjoining office, where Jayda, her effortlessly slender personal assistant, stood waiting.

"So," Jayda asked, glancing down at the iPhone in her hand. "What's the verdict? How much have you gained? And don't lie."

"I don't wanna talk about it."

"Don't do that, Gabby. The first step is acceptance. You gotta own that shit."

Pausing outside the restroom to step back into her dark green Manolo Blahnik platform shoes, Big Gabby shot her assistant an icy side-eye. Jayda folded her skinny arms across the incipient humps of her tiny breast and smiled. Her glossy dark hair was straight and shoulder-length, parted right down the middle. Her prescription eyeglasses added a mildly sophisticated edge to her cocoa brown visage. She wore a rose print off-the-shoulder minidress that was barely acquainted with her upper thighs and matching gray and white pumps with four-inch heels.

Big Gabby's dress was a shorter replica of the emerald green embellished column design Cynthia Erivo had worn back December. The 816 emeralds in her Audemars Piguet Royal Oak wristwatch accentuated the look, as did the weighty emeralds in her necklace and chandelier earrings. Although much of the strip club was festooned with all the pinks and reds that were essential and symbolic for the designated lovers' day, Big Gabby was all about the green, and tonight she planned to make plenty of it.

She went to her desk and lowered her voluminous rump onto the comfortable leather cushion of her swivel chair. It was a tight fit between the armrest, and the backrest creaked like old floorboards as she leaned back and stared at her beaming assistant.

The two black leather armchairs in front of Gabby's grand piano-sized desk were turned slightly towards each other, like a cheating husband discussing abortion with his pregnant mistress. Jayda sat down on the edge of one, crossed her legs, and said smilingly, "Okay. I get it. You're not in the mood to talk about it. Just know ta I'm here for you, girl."

"Don't get cute with me, Jayda."

"If I need advice on my weight, I'll hire a dietician."

Jayda dropped a sigh. Big Gabby stared straight at her, but Jayda's umber-colored eyes had already moved off to her right, to study framed photographs that graced the dark wood walls of Gabby's spacious first-floor office. The photos depicted Big Gabby standing side by side with some of the more famous women who'd visited Queen of Diamonds over the years. Chicago rap artist Dreezy, YoungNya, Fendi, Sahsa GoHard, Katie Got Bandz, and Shawnna. H-Town's Megan Thee Stallion and Miami's City Girls, Glorilla, Muni Long, Kash Doll, and Coi LeRay.

"You know *everybody,"* Jayda said, absentmindedly scratching an elbow as she gazed dreamily at the pictures. "Why you ain't got my auntie up there? She's one of the most famous porn stars in the game right now."

"Your auntie works here. She's a dancer. Maybe I'll put her up there when she moves on to something else, but while she's employed here? I'ma have to say no to that one."

Jayda Gordon was shaking her head even before Big Gabby was done speaking. "Nuh-uh. Nope. That ain't gon' work at all for me. BunnyXXX deserve a spot on your wall of fame, and if you won't put it up there I will."

Big Gabby dismissed the idea with a swift flick of the wrist as if she were swiping right on a dating app. Her gaze fell on the screen of the thirty inch Apple computer monitor on her massive oak desk. Blown up and split into four boxes on the screen were the live video images from the Prime Shift locker room just across the hall from Big Gabby's office the sprawling, the health and fitness spa that was further down the hall, the main locker room that connected to the health and fitness spa like an ugly conjoined twin, and the capacious Recruit and Training room, which occupied nearly half of the third floor.

The R& T room was deep, wide, and square, with solid white walls and sealed pine flooring. Thirty blue steel poles stood equidistantly apart, secured to the floor and ceiling with nuts and bolts, There was a dancer at every pole and two dozen more lingering near the mirror lined back wall, watching their fellow pole dancers spin and climb and drop into butt-jiggling splits. On one wall, a high narrow horizontal window allowed a long slat of westering sunlight to spill into the room.

In the health and fitness spa and both locker rooms, strikingly gorgeous young women of every brown hue tramped around in little more than thong underwear and heels, stretching and exercising and checking out all the new equipment, upgraded lockers, and swankier furnishings.

"Will there be a bunch of celebrities in the building tonight," Jayda asked.

"Absolutely." A fat smile lit up Gabby's pudgy face. "All twenty V.I.P. tables are already booked, and those were five thousand dollars a pop. We got performances from Twista, Do or Die, Bulletface, YoungNya, and Sicko Mobb. Princess and Alexus Costilla will be in V.I.P."

"Shut the front door! Queen A?" Jayda's eyes bulged behind the lenses of her gold framed spectacles.

Big Gabby nodded emphatically; her neck fat wobbled like brown Jello. "The one and only Johnna Broward's coming with her, so that's *two* black female *billionaires* we'll have in V.I.P. It can't get no better than that. Anybody who's somebody in the city will be in the building tonight, and you got front row seats to al the action."

"Front row seats," Jayda echoed, smiling like a fool on a stool. Her gaze became distant as she began to imagine how her night would unfold. Just eighteen years old she was a high school dropout from Kansas City, Missouri. "I've never met a famous person before. Closest thing to a celebrity I've seen up close was Shauntay Henderson."

Big Gabby furrowed her brow.

"Shauntay Henderson," Jayda repeated. "We're from the same hood. Twelfth Street, in Parker Square. That's the east side of K.C."

"What does Shauntay do? Is she a recording artist? An actress? What does she do?"

Jayda's bony shoulders rose and fell. "She's a gangster chick. Kinda like YoungNya. Only Shauntay didn't rap about what she did. She was on the FBI's Ten Most Wanted back in the day, right there with Ossama bin Laden and Whitey Bulger."

"Hm. Never heard of her."

"They say Princess Kelly used to be the same way before she got all rich and famous."

"She was," Big Gabby confirmed with a nod, " In fact, she pulled a gun on me right here in this office. Had one of the bouncers sneak it in to her through the back door. That's the reason I had the metal detector installed just inside that door during the renovations, Prinny's baby daddy was a notorious Black P. Stone from the South Side. He's in prison now, but that lifestyle stuck with her in a major way. She may have gone from stripping to being this big time TV star, but that street mentality is still in her. She'll fuck a bitch up in a heartbeat."

A small breath of air that might have been a light chuckle blew from Jayda's aquiline nose. Her eyeglasses skipped own the perfectly linear bridge of her nose, and she used the top of one index finger to push them back in place. Her eyes went to the ceiling, in search of the speakers that were currently playing one of Monica's throwback love ballads at medium volume.

"Speaking of bitches getting fucked up," the scantily clad nerd said, after a moment. "Are you at all concerned about Blicky and Shmoney coming to blows over that whole

Instagram beef they got going on? And what about Weezy's wife and kids? Didn't they just file a lawsuit against the company he signed QOD over to before he died? What if they show up on bullshit?"

"All that who owns-what-drama is between the Sullivan Family and Merrihill Equity Group. Weezy left the company to them, not me. I'm just the House Mom, and M.E.G is keeping me on as Chief Operating Officer for the time being," Big Gabby added, sliding open her bottom drawer and peering in at an obscenely large bag of Sour Patch Kids, "Weezy left all his money to his kids, over sixty million dollars. They're not thirsty enough to come in here fussing over ownership of the strip club. That'll stay between the lawyers—for now at least."

The big bag of sour gummy candies was screaming Gabby's name. She reached into the open drawer as if drawn in by some great magnetic force, and she might have given into the temptation had her iPhone not buzzed to life on her desk at that very moment. She shoved the drawer shut, exhaled a heavy breath, and momentarily closed her eyes in an effort to regain her composure.

"What about Blicky Nicky and Shmoney Rose?" Jayda asked. She was leaning in, trying to see who was calling her boss's phone.

"What about them?" Big Gabby picked up her phone to keep the nosey nerd at bay. "The MTN cameras will be in here filming. Whatever happens between them will only boost the ratings for that show and make Queen of Diamonds even more popular than it already is. Win-win."

Looking down at her phone, Gabby saw that the caller was her fiancé, veteran porn actor Tyrone Steele. It was a FaceTime video call, which she promptly answered.

Tyrone's head was like something you'd pick out of a box of Milk Duds; smooth, shiny and roundish in shape. Coasting through his middle forties like a man who could not age, Tyrone was tall and sturdily built, with dark, smoldering brown eyes and a sexy full lipped mirk that bewitched Gabby every time he flashed it her way.

"Hey, baby," he said, smirking.

The smile that came on Big Gabby's face rose from her mouth to her eyes and beyond.

"I...I, uhh...," she stammered.

A year and a half they'd been together, and still he had that effect on her.

Beads of perspiration trickled down his face and chest like rain on a windowpane. He was on his Peloton exercise bike, pedaling away in the corner of their living room. To his right, a huge glass window offered an awe-inspiring view of lake Michigan from forty-two stories up.

"You uhh what?"

Big Gabby giggled mischievously. "Nothing," she said; then, "I hope you're coming to see me at the club tonight. You know I won't be home until three of four in the morning."

"I'll be there long before that. Gotta support my baby." He was still pedaling. A rivulet of sweat went trailing down between his rippling pectoral muscles; watching it go, Big Gabby slipped her tongue out and used the tip of it to trace her upper lip from the left corner up and around to the right corner, like the hour hand on a clock going from three o'clock to nine o'clock in less than three seconds. "I got a little over a mile to go, and then I'll be in the shower and out the door," Tyrone continued. "Brick and his wife are coming with me. You think you can get us a table in the VIP section?"

"Wish I could." Big Gabby heaved a sigh of veritable regret. "They're all booked. Bankroll Reese snatched up the last table a little over an hour ago. If you stick around long enough, I'll get you to the first one that opens up. Those big names usually leave after an hour or so?"

Nodding and mopping his brow with the back of his waist, Tyrone said, "It's fine. I understand. I love you. I'll text you when I'm on my way."

"Love you more." Gabby considered telling him that she was now three hundred and one pounds, and that she was going to restart the monthly Ozempic injections she'd stopped taking after Weezy was killed, but Jayda's stare was too unwavering, too inquisitive, so instead of speaking Gabby puckered her lips and blew her man a kiss. Then she ended the call, looked at the time on her phone – 5:57 p.m. – and rose from her swivel, intentionally ignoring her smiling aide's relentless stare.

"You're engaged to that porn star," Jayda said; not a question, but a musical statement. "Auntie Bunny introduced you to him, didn't she? She told me she did."

Big Gabby crossed the room to the two cherrywood armoires that stood juxtaposed against the wall on the left side of the office.

"Get over here, Jayda." Gabby opened the doors on both armoires, revealing the vast collection of slutty clothing stowed within. "This is where I keep a lot of the outfits— thongs and bras and g-strings, fishnets and high heels— for the girls who either can't afford to buy their own or forget tiers at home. Keep track of all borrowed items. Don't let these bitches keep none of my shit, because they will."

Jayda walked up beside Big Gabby and nodded her head. She took a minute to thoroughly peruse her wardrobe, then turned her attention to Big Gabby and raked her eyes down the sparkling green Carolina Herrera dress.

"That dress is so nuke." Jayda commented.

"Nuke?"

"Yes, Nuke. Nuclear bomb, killing everything in a fifty mile radius. Look like somebody made it just for you."

"That's because it was made just for me. I met Wes Gordon at new York Fashion Week last year. He's the creative director at Carolina Herrera. I emailed him my measurements and a photo of Cynthia Eriva wearing a dress he designed for her that looked just like this one, and he made me this one. "

"It looks great on you. I know you're all worried over your weight, but I swear, you look good, and when I say good, I mean really, really good. I mean, you're what, five ten, five eleven? You're tall and you're not sloppy looking. You ain't got no big ole stomach. Yeah, you could maybe stand to lose a few pounds, but you look great. I mean that."

It was a rare event in Big Gabby's life when someone truly touched her heart and soul with the sheer warmth of their kind words. She wanted to shed a tear, but thinking better of it she smiled softly and said, "Thanks, I needed that. Go and get acquainted with the girls. Learn their names, their habits, their routines. Ask them if they need anything, and if they do note it in your phone. Nine times out of ten, if it's not in here—" She waved an arm at the open armoires "—it's in that utility closet at the far end of the hall."

"Got it." Jayda offered another nod. Her head was like a thumb onto which someone had drawn a face and planted a wig, a coffee-stained thumb. "Anything else?"

"No." Big Gabby closed the doors to her chic wooden armoires and went sauntering back to her desk. "I have a few emails to read and reply to and then I'll be out there with you. Text or call me if you have any problems."

"Got it," Jayda repeated.

She left hurriedly.

Stuffing her bountiful buttocks between the arms of her swivel chair, Big Gabby grabbed hold of her mouse, contemplated contacting her old personal trainer, and absentmindedly brought up the exterior camera images to see how many dancers had arrived since she last checked the parking lot.

All thoughts of rehiring John Byers disintegrated the instant she saw Blicky Nicky's shiny silver Tesla Cybertruck come cruising into the rear parking lot trailed by two black

SUVs. Sunlight glinted off the steel roof. Most of the snowfall had melted, leaving the asphalt dark and wet.

The row of yellow-lined parking slots just outside the back door was reserved for Big Gabby and the girls scheduled for Prime shift. If Gabby had possessed a weak heart, the sight of Blicky's Cybertruck pulling in three spaces to the right of her neon green Rolls Royce Spectre would have caused an infarction.

She expanded the camera image to full screen and then searched the other reserved parking slots for Shmoney Rose's hot-pink Bentayga. It was not present, but soon it would be. This harsh truth did nothing to soothe Big Gabby's pounding heart.

"Sweet baby Jesus," Gabby said, taking a big breath and blowing it out through pursed lips. "Take the wheel."

Chapter 5

Princess Kelly watched her handsome date with the right side of her mouth drawn back in a mildly hubristic grin. Her guests had arrived half an hour earlier – her childhood bestie Nishelle Dobbs and Nishelle's boyfriend, Keymo; her old friend Asia Mitchell and Nishelle's older brother Braylon; Aqua, Thick Doll, and Kimmy Kakes, women who'd gone from being Prinny's exotic dancing colleagues to her subordinates, depending on her for their paycheck; L-Stone and Monk, both of whom were Hyde Park Black P. Stones, just like Braylon and Keymo.

They were all gathered in Prinny's living room, a vast rectangular space with a twenty-foot ceiling, lacquered pine flooring, and three fat white leather sofas. A 212-inch widescreen TV that had cost Prinny $115,000 hung on the wall behind her like the screen in a movie theater, playing an episode of *The Chi*, on mute, while a BabyChiefDoit song blared from a pill-shaped speaker that stood in the middle of the glass top coffee table.

The single group had separated into three. Zoodie, who'd changed into a black silk button-down shirt with shimmery gold Versace designs all over it, was standing near the wide east entryway, sipping from his low ball glass of Hennessy and talking with the guys. Thick Doll was seated with Kimmy Kakes on the middle couch, their faces pressed together cheek to cheek while Kimmy held out her phone to snap a selfie. And branching off from Princess on either side were Asia, Aqua, and Nishelle.

"You won the whole game with that one over there," said Asia. Short and buxom, she was a dark chocolate little woman whose social graces seemed to extend no farther than creating some of the beautifully rolled blunts known to man, gulping down great mouthfuls of liquor, and formally introducing her teeth-scarred knuckles to the mouth of any woman who dared to look at her man for more than a millisecond. Now her inebriated gaze was fixed on Zoodie, and the corners of her mouth were raised in an approving smirk. "Oh yeah, You definitely won. That man is built like a .. like Trick Williams."

The four women tittered like schoolgirls. Asia was a big-time WWE fanatic and was always peppering their group chat with images of her favorite wrestlers in action. Rick Williams was one of them.

Aqua said, "So is this, like official? Are y'all together?"

"We're just friends," Prinny said with a toothy grin that conveyed the opposite. "I needed a date to go with me to QOD, so I flew him out here for the date."

"He done got flewed out." Asia laughed, and her laughter spread quickly to the others, like the first strain of Covid-19. She had her weave fashioned into at thick black braid that went down past the butt of her tight red pants. "I bet any amount of money that you put him up in First Class, too. Didn't you?"

Prinny's guilt silence invoked another bout of guffaws.

"Whatever the case may be," Aqua said when the laughter died down, "I'm just glad that you found somebody to date. And I'm *too* glad it ain't Grind or Marko. I told you the night we met Zoodie that you should've pursued something serious with him. A man that fine only comes along once in a lifetime."

"Enough about me and what I got goin' on." Vexed by the intense focus on her personal life, Princess moved the conversation in another direction. To Aqua she said, "Tell me what happened when y'all went over there to talk to Blicky."

"*That* bitch," Aqua exclaimed. She then went on to recount her and Thick Doll's delightfully entertaining visit to Blicky Nicky's west side home

Midway through the story the four of them migrated to the sofa so Thick Doll could give her take on the Blicky encounter. Every one of them had a drink in hand. Aqua had just finished telling them about Blicky Nicky's witty *Nutty Professor* rap when Princess looked over and noticed that Nishelle had not taken so much as a taste of her Hennessy. There was a troubled look in Shell's eyes, but her smile and mood were incongruously cheerful. She kept checking her iPhone. Someone was texting her like crazy.

Princess leaned in to talk in Nishelle's ear. "Sis, you good? Why you ain't drinkin'?"

"I'm fine."

"You sure?"

"Yeah," Nichelle's thick lips parted to say something else, but then she closed them, sighed, and a moment later repeated. "Yeah."

That oddly cheerful smile remained, but it twitched at the corners, as if some invisible man's unsteady fingertips were holding it in place. Princess reacted to the twitch; her honey brown eyes went asquint, and she tilted her head to the side so that the fat diamond hoop of her earring brushed lightly at the shoulder of her black and red Balenciaga bodysuit. She took in a long, slow deep breath, pulling fresh oxygen into her lungs and bloodstream. On the exhale she stood up, balancing herself on the six inch heels of her black spiked Louboutin ankle boots like a veteran circus performer on stilts. She made a come hither gesture with her index finger and left the room with Shell trailing behind her. From the corner of her eye she saw that the men turned their heads to ogle her fat round ass and Shell's even fatter round ass as the two of them went sauntering past.

Nishelle Dobbs was twenty-four years old and built like London "Deelish" Charles, and she'd been that way since she was fourteen. The complexion of her skin was not unlike the amber liquid slashing to and fro in her glass. She wore a form-fitting black leather dress with a plunging neckline that made her big perky breasts seem as if they might spill out at any given moment. She was a chef who'd honed her culinary chops in France before returning to the Chi to open her own restaurant, The Plate, in the Lake View neighborhood just north of Lincoln Park. Prinny had invested a full million dollars into the business, which made her the forty-nine percent minority owner of The Plate, while Shell owned the controlling fifty-one percent share.

Prinny led her friend and business partner down a wide hallway with blue marble tile flooring and heavy oak doors on either side. Here the air was fresher than in the living room. The sounds their high heels made on the marble tiles brought to mind a quartet of grandfather clocks, all of them ticking and rocking in rhythmic fashion, neither of them in sync with the others.

One door on the left opened into a private theater with black carpeting on the floor and walls, sixteen overstuffed black leather recliners, and a huge silver screen on the front wall that played *Renaissance: A Film by Beyonce* on a continuous loop. Nineteen minutes and forty-two second into the record-breaking concert documentary, Princess and her five-year-old daughter Vee could be seen smiling and waving their hands in the air in the very front row at the United Center.

She stepped into the theater room, nursing her cognac through a short red straw as Shell came in behind her and pushed the door shut. Shell replied to a text message. Then she stowed her phone in the bodice of her dress and pincered her forehead between her thumb and middle finger. When she finally looked up at Prinny she had tears glimmering on her eyes.

"I'll... I'll deal with it," Shell said, her voice fragmenting under the pressure of whatever was weighing down on her.

"She's just high. I know what it. She's high out of her mind. Tramell got her smokin' that chemical bullshit, all those kids are probably driving her up the wall, and you know what? I bet he put it in her head to begin with."

Prinny sipped at her drink and said nothing. She was waiting for the meat of the stew to rise to the surface. Tramell Johnson was Nishelle's cousin Sadé's boyfriend and the father of two of her six children. Sadé owned a somewhat dilapidated four bedroom house near the corner of 54th Street and Hayne Avenue. She'd met Tramell just a few days before he nationwide Covid-19 lockdown was put in place. At the time Tramell was living on campus at the University of Chicago, around 54th and Ellis Avenue. Sadé had driven past in her cream colored Ford Taura and seeing Tramell jogging along the sidewalk with is head lowered against the rain, she'd offered him a ride. They'd been inseparable ever since.

Back then Sadé had been a part of Prinny's inner circle. In fact, Sadé's place had been the main hangout spot for their lady gang. Prinny still remembered that rainy evening when Sadé left on a store run for blunts, hamburger buns, and toilet paper, only to return with the homely young black man who would soon drive a wedge between her and the rest of the gang.

Prinny hated Tramell with the passion of Christ.

"You bet he put what in her head?" The right side of Prinny's upper lip rose in a contemptuous sneer as she voiced the question.

Shell inhaled sharply through her nose in what could only be described as a nasal sigh in reverse. "Okay," she said, and ran her hand down her face. "Okay listen. And don't get mad. I was gonna tell you this tomorrow anyway, I just didn't want to ruin your night out with the girls. It's been forever since we all got together and really enjoyed ourselves."

"Girl, if you don't start talkin'..."

Shell turned and began pacing the length of the aisle that led to the back of the room, where two identical popcorn machines stood on either side of the film projector at the rear wall. There was an upward slant going that way, like in a real theater, and it took Shell maybe twenty-two steps to make it there and back. She raised her drink as she walked and, grimacing, chugged it down in three fat swallows.

"Okay," She began, after another reverse sigh, "Okay, So, uh, you remember when, after your baby daddy got arrested for dealing to that confidential informant, he mailed you the paperwork showing that it was Gutterville Slim who set him up?"

Prinny gave a slow, reluctant nod. Her mouth went dry, and she knew it wasn't a delayed reaction to the four blunts of exotic weed she'd smoked with her girls. It was the anxiety-inducing fear of what Nishelle might say next that drained all the moisture from her tongue.

"Well," Shell said, turning at the rear of the aisle and heading back toward Prinny, "according to Sadé you hit her up a few days after you got that paperwork, asked her to help you set Slim up to get killed and you would pay off the seventy-seven hundred she owed on the house her grandma left her. You knew her first baby daddy was one of Slim's boys from Gutterville. She took you to one of their parties at some girls house on Damen, you called L-Stone and Mike Moe to come and get Slim, and when Sadé tried to leave before they got there you went out to his car and finessed him into giving you a ride home. She ain't sure what happened after that, all she knows is that Slim was found dead in his car two blocks over from her house a few hours later, and when she got home she found you sitting on her couch watching a G Herbo music video, with all seventy-seven hundred dollars of the blood money piled up on the coffee table in front of you. That's what she calls it. The blood money."

And she accepted it, Prinny thought, but she didn't dare say it. Saying such a thing would veritably imply guilt.

So instead she said, "That girl done lost her mind."

"Let her tell it, the whole situation is what's *making* her lose her mind. Slim's son goes to school with her kids, and I guess he's been … somebody's been abusing him. His stepdad. The boy came to school earlier this week with a broken nose and three broken ribs. The stepdad was arrested for child abuse, but he'll be back on the streets in a week or so. Sadé feels like it's her fault. She wants to go down to the police station and confess to her involvement in Slim's murder. To right her wrongs. And that dumb fuck Tramell is urging her to do it."

"Are you fuckin' serious?" Prinny was furious for a second or two, but her fury had dissipated by the time her disbelief was communicated. The anger turned to apprehension. If Sadé went to the police with everything she knew about Slim's unsolved murder, there was a very real possibility that Princess Kelly would end up charged and convicted.

"I know, Prinny, I know." Nishelle had stopped pacing. She stood three feet away from Prinny, looking slightly taller than unusual standing farther up the incline. "Just give me some time, okay? A day or two. Give me a day or two. Let me talk to her. She'll listen to me. She   always listens to me."

"What if I don't   have a day or two, Nichelle?" Huh? Have you considered that? What if that bitch is on her way to the police station as we speak?" Her hand was on the bronze doorknob before the latter question mark fell off her parched tongue. She flung the door open with such force that, had Shell been standing two feet closer, it likely would have knocked her all the way back to the popcorn maker at the far end do the aisle.

Their heels connected with the cobalt blue marble tiles like grandfather clocks on Adderall on their way back to the living room, Prinny taking long, angry strides and Shell sprinting to keep up with her.

"I'm tellin' you right now, Nishelle, if you ever in life keep a secret like that from me again, some shit that could literally fuck up my whole life, it's gon' me and you."

"I'm sorry, Prinny. I just don't want her getting hurt."

"*I don't want her getting hurt*," Prinny echoed in a low mocking intonation. "What about *me* gettin' hurt? What about the possibility of my daughter losing *both* her parents to that crooked ass *in*justice system? Did you think about that?" She wagged her head in frustration. "Of course you didn't"

"If L-stone finds out about this he'll have her hurt. You know it like I know it. I can't take that risk. At the end of the day she's still my cousin."

Prinny made no reply. She understood Nishelle's innate fear of L-Stone's wrath. The dread-headed villain was a General of the Almighty Black P. Stones, one of Chicago's most savage Black street gangs. When he poured salt on someone's name and reputation, it was never long before that unfortunate someone was found balled up like a salted slug, with more holes in their chest and skull than a cheese grater. But that very rational fear was beside the point. Prinny and Shell were lifelong besties. Loyalty trumped fear three-to-one. At least in Prinny's book it did.

When they reentered the living room everyone but Kimmy Kakes was seated on the sofas and Kimmy – nearing forty and aging like a fine Black American wine – had the floor. Baby ChiefDoIt's *Animal Only* mixtape had segued into Lil Durk's *Deep Thoughts* album, and someone had lowered the volume on that. Asia's thin lips were folded in over her teeth to hold the blunt she was trying to light with her black plastic lighter, L-Stone and Keymo were counting through foot-high piles of crisp new hundreds, and Kimmy was regaling the seated menagerie of well-dressed friends with the story of the night she had teamed up with Thick Doll and Aqua to offload twenty kilos of cocaine to some Kankakee dope boy called Donny the Don.

"The shit didn't go sideways until *after* the drug deal," Kimmy was saying as she stood there on the opposite side of the coffee table from her audience, a coffee table that was really just an octagonal block of cobalt blue marble with a large avid slab of glass laid over it. "We had already counted up all the cash, Donny and his lil crew had already left with their twenty bricks or whatever. Aqua had the brilliant idea of offering Fat Perry five thousand dollars to hold security for us during the drug deal, so his thirsty ass got to watch us run over a half a million dollars through the money counters..."

Prinny knew the rest of the story by heart. Fat Perry, who at the time was employed as a bouncer at Queen of Diamonds, had put a gun to Aqua's face and demanded she give him fifty grand instead of the five he was owed. Either that or he'd take it all. Aqua had kindly informed him that if he took a single dollar he'd be taking from Millionaire Markio, a ranking member of the Traveling Vice lords street gang with long money and a mercilessly short temper. The fat man had backed off after that, but the drama hadn't ended there. They were in their respective vehicles preparing to leave the K-Town neighborhood in which the drug deal took place- the girls in Aqua's coke white Navigator, Fat Perry in his bruise=colored Buick sedan— when two or three gunmen leapt out of a brown van and opened fire on the phalanx of gang members. Thick Doll had called over to stand outside and make sure Donny didn't try anything funny. Aqua had sideswiped Fat Perry's car in her haste to escape the gun battle, knocking his front end loose in a real accident that only served to infuriate him even further.

Prinny tuned out the histrionic narrative and all the gasps and laughs it evoked. Her daughter, Vonzella, would be six this year. All she wanted for her birthday was to take that hours long drive to Menard Correctional Center so she could visit with her imprisoned father, Vee was a beautiful brown girl with a precociously inquisitive nature and a smile more infections than any communicable disease.

And what would happen to that bright-eyed smile if Vee were to find herself with *two* incarcerated parents?

Princess didn't want to think about it.

She picked up her iPhone from one of the end tables and used it to FaceTime a woman whose army of cartel soliders just south of the U.S./Mexican border mad L-stone and his gang seem like Boy Scouts.

"I'm getting ready now," Alexus Costilla answered. The stunningly attractive black-and-Mexican business mogul had her left eye shut, and a makeup artist was applying a thin layer of bronze eyeshadow to the closed lid. Behind her a hairstylist was tending to her long dark hair. The white of her right eye was the canvas for a roadmap of dark red veins that led to a lively green iris and dilated pupil. "Nya's coming too. Her, Noesha, Quita Hales-they're all coming." She exhaled heavily. "I'm so fucking high right now. So high I don't know what to do."

The hairstylist giggled.

From somewhere off camera Alexus's stepdaughter, Savaria King, shouted, "I'm coming! We're celebrating! Ma, tell her the news we just got!"

"She just got accepted into Harvard. You know that's my mom's alma mater." Alexus shot a proud look to the right of the screen. "This little brat finally did it."

"Yup. I sure did," Vari quipped. "And I want that pink Bugatti you promise me, the one you got at the house in Matamoros. You told me I could get it if I got accepted into Harvard. Time to pay up."

Alexus rolled her right eye just as the cosmetologist finished coating her left eyelid. Looking at Princess again, she said, "You see the shit I have to put up with? This is an everyday thing with her, with King, with Juan. All three of my kids are spoiled rotten."

Despite her troubled state of mind, Prinny found the left side of her mouth rising in the tiniest semblance of a smirk. Here she was fretting over a potential life sentence, and Queen A's daughter was griping over a two-million-dollar car she'd been promised. That was the funny thing about being friends with the wealthiest Black woman (well, *half* Black woman) in world history. The current wealthiest person on the planet according to *Forbes and Bloomberg*, was Elon Musk, with a reported $400 billion, and Alexus was hot on his heels with her $317 billion.

"I'd hate to ruin the mood," Prinny said, speaking low to keep the party out of her business, "but we got a problem. A big one."

The prideful smile on Queen A's gorgeous face fled so fast it could have been a figment of Prinny's imagination. A look of cautious uncertainty replaced that expression.

"What do you mean? What kind of problem?"

"Can't talk about it over the phone, but it's serious. I'll uh… I'll probably be late getting to the club. Gotta take care of something else first. I'll tell you all about it when I get to QOD."

She ended the call before Alexus could ask any more questions and turned to Shell, whose face held an expression of mental constipation. Which seemed fitting. She'd been holding shit in that should have been let out. She leaned in toward Princess and whispered, "Please don't tell L-stone about this. She's my blood, Prinny."

Princess made no reply. She waited for Kimmy Kakes to end the thrilling story and then said, "Okay, okay, okay. Everybody up. We're rollin' out. Got one stop to make on Fifty-fourth and Hayne, then it's to the stirp club we go."

There were cheers all around.

Chapter 6

"We are officially video vixens," Jaresha said joyfully.

"We is, ain't we?" Tammy sounded just as electrified. "I honestly didn't think Nya would be that cool. She ain't let all that money and fame go to her head."

"Definitely didn't"

The two of them were descending from the red-carpeted staircase that ended approximately three feet from the red steel back door exit to The Visionary Lounge. Triple rows of fluorescent tubes lined the ceiling, thoroughly illuminating the stairwell. A thick black rug lay on the smooth gray concrete floor just inside the doorway. The rug had *T.V.L.* printed on it in big, bold gold lettering, and there was a five-pointed star resting on the inner curvature of a golden crescent moon above the V.

Nya and her entourage were coming down the stairs too, though they had yet to round the corner of the second floor landing eight or nine steps above and behind Jaresha and Tammy. Their loud, intoxicated voices carried down easily; they'd been drinking all throughout the video shoot. Nya was telling her girls— Noesha, Iyanna, Shaquita, and another pretty girl with pink hair and high cheekbones whose name Jaresha couldn't remember— about an argument she'd had with her boyfriend, Young Meach, after she caught him cozying up to a dancer on the set of one of his video shoots. Like Nya, Meach was a rap artist, and also like Nya, he was signed to Money Bagz Management.

Commenting on Nya's relationship problems, Tammy said, in a voice so low it was barely a whisper, "I wouldv'e fucked the shit outta Meach if I was that dancer."

Jaresha choked back a laugh and just about stumbled down the last two steps. Had she been wearing heels she'd have almost certainly fallen down. She'd been tossing back shots like the rest of the girls and was a bit unsteady on her feet. Fortunately for her she was a Air Jordan girl and wore the number elevens tied snugly on her small, pretty feet. The sneakers were black and red, her low-rise jeans were so dark gray they wanted to be black, and her puffy Louis Vuitton jacket was the black her jeans aspired to be. Her fingernails were jet-black claws. Even her lipstick was black. It was her favorite color.

"Where did he go?" Tammy pointed at a vacant, blue steel fold-out chair in a wide niche just across from the staircase. The security guard who'd seen them in had gone there to sit as they were climbing the stairs. His bottle of Fiji water and the paperback novel he'd had his fat black thumb wedged in – K'wan's *Hood Rat* – were on the floor next to the chair, but the huge black man had left his post.

With a careless shrug, Jaresha shoved open the heavy red door and sauntered out into an eddy of cold, refreshing air. The sun had left the horizon, and the sky was deep blue sea rolling across the heavens. There were maybe a dozen vehicles in the parking lot, most of them presumably owned or rented by members of the music video production crew. Someone had parked a SUV in the space next to Jaresha's G-Wagon.

It was a dark-colored Ford Explorer, ad it was parked facing away from the club. A sticker on the tinted rear window warned that its occupants were die-hared Chicago Sky Fans. The bumper looked a little loose. Two short strips of duct tape held the driver's side taillight in place.

"I know I better get some kinda role in yo' lil scary movie when they start filmin' it," Tammy said as she headed around to the G-Wagon's passenger side.

Jaresha opened her mouth and what nearly came out was: *We won't even need to use prosthetics on your ugly-ass face.*

The shit-eating grin that would have accompanied the witty remark was just beginning to form when both doors of the Explorer's driver's side flew open. The driver rushed at Jaresha and pressed the barrel of his semi-automatic pistol against her jaw. At the edge of her vision she saw his partner go running after Tammy, and she heard Tammy's terrified gasp when the man reached her, but the only gunman Jaresha was truly focused on was the one standing right in front of her.

The first thing she noticed about him was that they were the exact same height, five seven, and the second was that his breath smelled like spoiled chitterlings. This latter revelation came when he spoke.

"Don't make me shoot cho sexy ass," he said from behind a poorly groomed mop of dreadlocks. His free hand smacked down onto her collarbone and closed into a fist with a handful of her jacket balled up inside it. "Long as you listen, you'll be a'ight. Step back here. And don't try no dumb shit."

She tried not to grimace at the exceedingly bad smell emanating from his rotten mouth and failed worse than Aubrey in his famous war of words with Kendrick.

He yanked her toward the rear of her G-Wagon and she went stumbling in that direction.

"Don't try no dumb shit," he reiterated, dragging her along. "This pipe got a switch on it. One lil squeeze it'll chop yo' whole lil head off. Thirty shots in one second."

Jaresha knew that it actually would take two seconds for a Glock pistol modified with a fully auto switch to deplete a 30-round magazine, but this was no time to argue semantics.

He shoved her against the back of her Mercedes and took two purposeful steps back just as his taller, skinnier partner came around from the passenger side holding Tammy by the throat. Jaresha looked down and saw the door security guy keeling beside her with his back to the gunmen and his hands behind his balding head; he was too fat, and his arms were too short for his pudgy fingers to interlace, but his fingertips were touching. The side pockets of his dark blue trousers were turned inside out, and the gold watch he'd worn on his right wrist was gone.

The robber with the fecal matter marinating in his throat aimed his gun at Jaresha's chest. "Strip," he commanded as if prompting a dog to perform some amazing trick.

"Don't do us like that. Please don't," Jaresha implored. She began unfastening her own watch. "Y'all see this? It's an Audemars. Cost me a hundred and twelve thousand dollars, and that was before my jeweler put all the diamonds in it. Here, take it."

She tossed the blinging diamond timepiece to Mr. Shit Breath and he spent a moment admiring the exorbitant wristwear before raising it to show his masked compadre.

The tall man's mask concealed every part of his head but his eyes, making him look like a ninja in a yellow hoodie and jeans. He kept his pistol—a bulky chrome revolver—trained on Tammy while he turned to study the watch.

Jaresha's heart was a coked-up drummer boy in the marching band of her chest. Her fingers played imaginary pianos at her sides. Clasped around her neck was a Cuban-link necklace with a VVS diamond incrustation and a big diamond pendant that spelled out her stage name, Kitty Jae, above a fat, smiling kitten. The chain and pendant were worth even more than her watch. To combat the cold she'd zipped her jacket all the way up to her throat, effectively concealing the gaudy piece of jewelry, but if the robber made her strip, her necklace was as good as gone.

The facade of The Visionary Lounge faced Chicago Avenue, were a dense flow of vehicular traffic moved east and west through the evening twilight. Off to the east side of the towering yellowstone nightclub, on Laramie, a lengthy queue of cars and trucks idled at the red light, waiting for it to turn gren so they could continue on their respective journeys.

But in the dimly-lit parking lot behind The Visionary Lounge, where Jaresha stood defenseless with a modified Glock aimed at her sternum, there were no curious pedestrian or motorist around to witness what was taking place. A local older woman had petitioned the city to shut down TVL and revoke its license to serve alcohol following a spate of shootings on and around the premises and the court had ordered the owner to essentially press pause on his highly lucrative business while the court proceedings were underway. The club owner—mn a dapper young man called Bankroll Reese— had allowed Nya and her team inside for the express purposes of filming her music video.

"Nah," Shit Breath said finally. He pocketed the watch, but there must have been a hole in the pocket of his beige Adidas sweat pants, because the watch went plummeting down his inner pantleg. Suprised, he looked down, "The fuck?" He stuck his hand in the pocket and shook it around in disbelief. "Damn, Rock," he said, turning to his partner in crime. "Got a hole in my pocket."

The yellow-hooded ninja gave him a hard look. "That ain't' my name, man."

"Yes it is."

"*No it ain't!* And why the fuck you ain't put the mask on?"

"I told you on the last lick, the shit make my face sweat, and I get all claus... claus... whatever the word is when yo hate bein' in closed spaces." He bent forward and crouched a little, reaching down in his pants for the watch. His shoes, Jaresha noted were black Cortezes white smudge brown Nike swooshes that might have been white once. The sole on the left one drooped at the front like an unhappy lip. "And nigga," he said, rising with the watch in hand and momentarily lowering his gun, "since when yo' name change? You been Rock ever since I met you."

The ninja named Rock tilted his head forward, closed his eyes and took a deep breath.

An incipient smirk of amusement creased the corner of Jaresha's mouth, but only for a second, because when Rock lifted his head there was a murderous rage in his eyes that snipped all hilarity from the moment.

"Listen man," Rock said, clearly struggling to contain his rage. "That's Kitty Jae. She should have that chain on. Get it so we can go."

They knew about my chain? Jaresha thought. She looked down to see whether her jacket was open or not. It was not. So how did they know what she had on underneath it? She wondered.

"Why you all over here?" Shit Breath snapped at Rock. "Ain't you supposed to be robbin' that skinny bitch?" he waved his gun at Tammy. "I got this over here. Always tryna tell me what to do. Just 'cause I got a baby by yo' sister don't mean you my big brotha. Ny can't tell me what to do, and *you* can't neither."

The kneeling security guy snorted a chuckle.

Tammy's mouth fell open, and she muttered under her breath, "He cannot possibly be that stupid."

In a shocking turn of events— or perhaps not-so-shocking, considering the sheer ignorance displayed by the bare-faced robber who seemed to have eaten a hot bowl of diarrhea for dinner— Rock turned his gun on Shit Breath and said, 'Shutt. The fuck. Up."

So Shit Breath aimed his gun at Rock.

"Or what? Shut the fuck up, or what? I got thirty rounds in this muhfucka, nigga, and you got six. That means I got *ten* times as many bullets as you got. So how you wanna do dis?"

A tense standoff ensued. It was fleeting, lasting just four or five seconds, certainly no longer than six, but it seemed to span eons. An icy breath of a breeze swept through the parking lot and sent an empty Flamin' Hot Cheetos bag cartwheeling across the damp asphalt. Jaresha's wide eyes moved from Shit Breath to Rock and back to Shit Breath again. The rolls of fat at the nape of the security guy's neck changed shape as he twisted around to get a glimpse of the showdown. Silently, Tammy mouthed, Oh my God.

Then the back door exit to The Visionary Lounge banged open. Nya and her girlfriends emerged in a glorious whirlwind of laughter and conversation, and the standoff ended as suddenly as it began.

Shit Breath and Rock abandoned their robbery mission and hopped back in their Explorer. Tires churning, they shot out of the parking lot, swung a hard left onto Laramie, and disappeared north.

"We just got robbed!" Tammy yelled as she ran off to join Nya's entourage fifteen feet away.

Jaresha stayed to help the big man to his feet. She supported his left elbow in both hands and lifted, while he pressed the palm of his right hand against her license plate and hoisted himself upright.

"That whole thing was set up," he said, bending to massage his wet and undoubtedly aching knees. "They came to rob you. Followed you here. I heard em' talkin' about it 'fore you came out."

"Yeah, I figured that out when, uhhh, Rock, when Rock mentioned my necklace." Jaresha directed a wary glance toward Laramie Ave. The light had turned green sometime during the standoff and now she could see clear across to the gas station on the opposite corner. She realized that she was breathing shakily and forced herself to take several long, slow, measured breaths. "I don't know how they could've even found out that I had this chain on. I left my house and picked New-New up from the airport, dropped my sister off

60

at her boyfriend's house, and then drove here for the video shoot."

The big man looked at the men and women who had exited the club with Nya and were now surrounding her and Tammy in a protective circle. Two of them had drawn handguns from under their sweatshirts and were surveying the area in case the robbers returned. Noesha was outside the circle, arms folded across her chest, regarding Jaresha with concerned eyes.

"Any one of those girls over here named Tammy?" The big guy asked the question in a low, conspiratorial tone.

Jaresha's head jerked back on her neck, and she furrowed her brow as she looked up at him. He was tall, wide, and fat, reminding her of Bruce Bruce, the comedic legend of Comic View Fame. His head appeared to be resting directly on top of his shoulders, with nary a neck to support it.

"Yeah," Jaresha said with her mouth hanging open. "Why?"

"Because." Bruce Bruce leaned his heavy bulk against the side of her boxy Mercedes SUV and exhaled at the steadily darkening sky. "When that dumb nigga had the gun to my head, takin' all my shit, the smarter one got a phone call. Whoever was on the other end told him to rob Kitty Jae for her watch and chain, but to make sure he didn't take nothin' from Tammy. Was that her standing' next to me a minute ago? The skinny bitch with the fat ass?"

Jaresha said nothing. For a short while she stood there staring up at the inquisitive brown giant with her mouth and eyes agape and her head canted slightly to the side.

"Kitty, you good girl?"

It was Noesha, and there was tangible worry in her voice as she came walking toward Jaresha.

Jaresha shook her head and then turned it to stare mutely at her approaching friend. Aside from that small movement she remained frozen in place. She told her legs to move, to go to New-New and embrace her, but at first, they wouldn't obey the signal her brain was sending them. When they finally did start working New-New was just two or three feet away. They embraced, and again Noesha asked if Jaresha was good, but all Jaresha did was look past Noesha's left shoulder to stare at the cousin of hers who she was pretty sure had just set her up to be robbed.

Chapter 7

Queen of Diamonds officially reopened for business at seven o'clock p.m. Big Gabby had initially planned an elaborate ribbon-cutting ceremony, mainly to show out for the MTN cameras she'd allowed inside to film the Prime Shift dancers Prinny had selected as cast members for her hit reality show, but she'd ultimately canned the idea. Weezy hadn't cut any ribbons when he first opened the upscale strip joint. He had lingered just inside the second set of front doors in his Brioni suit and tie, greeting the incoming patrons with warm hugs and firm handshakes, all the while beaming his magnanimous, open-mouthed smile.

So Big Gabby stood where Weezy had stood on that monumental evening years prior, and she behaved in similar fashion, though her smile came in the form of closed lips unless there were words to accompany it.

Several notable faces stuck out in the welcomed herd of clubgoers. Among them were social media influencers, Instagram models, TikTok stars, locally renowned business owners, rap artists, two R&B songstresses, and seven or eight pro athletes from the NBA and NFL. Big Gabby directed most of these very important people to the elevated VIP Lounge, which was roped off and guarded by burly black bouncers at the foot and head of both winding staircases. The sofas up there had been reupholstered in a velvety fabric the color of deep red wine, as had the sofas and chairs on the main floor. A festoonery of pink and red Valentine's Day ballons clung to the walls and ceiling fixtures. Lizzo's "Tempo" featuring Missy Elliott pulsed through the building, its pounding bassline infusing the sexy young strippers with all the energy they needed to go hard.

By seven forty-five the strip club was filled almost to capacity. Only a couple of VIP tables remained untouched, and that was only because they were reserved for celebrity guests who had yet to arrive. Every stool at the L-shaped bar was taken, dollar bills were flying all over the place, and the air was thick with the strong aroma of weed smoke.

Queen of Diamonds was back in business.

"This is so fuckin' nuke," Jayda said, shouting so that Big Gabby could hear her over the music. "Hands down, this is already the most exciting night of my life. It can only go up from here."

Big Gabby put her arm around Jayda's shoulders and pulled her close for a smiling couple of seconds. They were standing near the north transept of the cross-shaped main stage, which rose three feet and two inches above the floor. The Preferred Shift dancer who was kneeling on the stage in front of them, making her meaty brown buttocks jump one cheek at a time, was called Drips. She had big eyes, short blond hair, and a tattoo of an infant's giggling face on her right shoulder. Her sharply pointed fingernails were silver like the sequins on her seven-inch stripper heels. She was bouncing her ass to the beat of Latto's "Brokey" while the men standing around her end of the stage showered her with dollars.

"You just keep an eye on that phone," Big Gabby shouted back at her teenage assistant. "If Blicky Nicky moves one inch off that sofa, you let me know."

Jayda looked down at the phone she was holding in her right hand. It was Big Gabby's iPhone. On the screen was an image from the high definition camera bolted high in one corner of the Prime Shift locker room, which was just across the hallway from Gabby's office. At first glance it appeared to be a still image, as neither of the two eight-inch televisions were on and Blicky Nicky was sitting forward on the plush red U-shaped sofa with her hands steepled together and her head lowered, as if in prayer. But it was indeed a live video feed; upon closer examination, Jayda could see that Blicky's right leg was bouncing vigorously, and since her elbows were resting on her knees, the continuous bounce was transferred to her steepled fingers. No one else was in the Prime Shift locker room – which was much more spacious and grand than the one all the other dancers had to use – because Prime Shift didn't begin until 10:00 p.m.

Big Gabby watched Drips perform for another minute or two and then moved on, working the room in House Mom mode, checking on her dancers and bartenders and black-shirted bouncers. Jayda kept pace beside her, duly noting the employees' wants and needs on her own iPhone. The bartenders were beautiful and curvy enough to be strippers themselves, and one of them, a gray-eyed, light skinned stunner called Trixie, complained that there weren't enough paper towels behind the bar to keep up with the liquor spillage, and no trash can to drop them into. Adonis, a dark, 6' 5" bouncer with an Herculean physique and Grecian features, told Gabby that one of the toilets in the men's restroom wouldn't stop flushing. A bottle girl named Tasha snitched that another bottle girl whose first name was the same as hers was drinking on the job.

Tasha had just finished tattling on her namesake when a nicely built young woman with the unfortunate face of a dark brown ogre got up from a nearby sofa and walked over to Gabby. She was dressed in a light blue Fendi catsuit and even lighter blue high-heeled boots that boosted her height to somewhere around 5'11" (which was Gabby's natural height without heels).

Big Gabby recognized the woman as her ex-boss's eldest daughter. She'd never met the girl in person, and she didn't know her name, but she'd seen her on Weezy's social media over the years. The girl had a facial resemblance to her father that Gabby found deeply unsettling. She got really close to Gabby, invading the House Mom's personal space, the tip of her bulbous nose nearly making contact with Gabby's bottom lip.

"How'd you get him to do it?" The woman tipped her head sideways and squinted with her question. Her faux lashes were too long and too stiff, like slanting black needles growing out from her eyelids. "That's all I wanna know."

"Uhhh.. Do I know you?" Gabby asked, feigning ignorance. She used her fingertips to gently push the girl back a step, lowering her hand before the girl could swipe the pressing fingers from the shoulder.

"You know damn well who I am. Deona Sullivan. Weezy was my daddy."

More like Fiona, Big Gabby thought, studying the girl's bloated, Shrek-like visage, which looked oddly out of place above such a gorgeous body. It was as if someone had lopped off Princess Fiona's ugly green head, dyed it brown, and sewed it onto Amer Rose's neck

"So tell me," Implored the bodacious-bodied ogre. "How'd you get my daddy to sign over ownership of his strip club, his pride and fuckin' joy, to you? And just hours before he was killed, at that. How'd you do it? Our lawyer had a handwriting professional look at the signature, and he claims it's legit."

"You've been misinformed," Gabby said. "Your father didn't sign over anything, he sold it, and he didn't sell it to me, he sold it to Merrill Equity Group."

Leona clucked her tongue off the roof of her mouth and wagged her forefinger. "Uh-uh. Nope. You see, we got ourselves a *good* lawyer, one of the best in the game. Ezekeil Pratt. He interned at Bostic and Staples for two whole years before leaving to start his own practice. He knows all the tricks of the trade, and he saw right through your whole little scheme."

"There is no scheme. As I said you've been mis—"

"—informed," Deona finished for Gabby. "Sure. That's what it was. Pure misinformation. Fake news." She nodded her ugly round head. Her eyelashes didn't budge. "So tell me this, Big Gabby, tell me this and I'll shut my mouth and leave you to go on proudly welcoming all these folks to the strip club y'all stole from my daddy right before he died in that explosion."

Big Gabby planted her hands on the hips of her dazzling green dress and breathed like she was practicing yoga. Adonis caught sight of the burgeoning confrontation and started toward it from eight tables away, his overly muscled legs propelling him in long, powerful strides. Five feet behind Deona, perched on the soft crimson sofa she'd gotten up from, were three young men who looked a lot like her. They wore expensive-looking business suits with shirts that were unbuttoned and spread open to reveal their diamond necklaces.

A family of well-dressed ogres.

"You're right about Merrill Equity Group owning the place," Deona continued. "But who owns Merrihill Equity Group? That's the ten-million-dollar question, ain't it?"

Big Gabby opened her mouth to say *I'm only part-owner of M.E.G.* but she saw that one of the male ogres had raised his cell phone to capture video of the exchange, so she brought her lips back together in a derisive smile, took in another deep yoga breath, and kindly said, "You have a nice night."

She was walking away with Jayda and Adonis flanking her when Deona yelled. "Oh, I will! I'ma have me a good ol' night! and I'ma have an even nicer day in court!"

Chapter 8

54th and Hoyne was Ganster Disciple territory.

Prinny's entourage of Black P. Stones and the Gangster Disciples were sworn enemies, had been since way back in the days of Jeff Fort and Larry Hoover.

That being said, it came as no surprise when L-Stone had his boys climb out of the second Mercedes Sprinter van with their pistols in hand.

The two Sprinters – blacked-out and armored with bulletproof windows and Teflon=layered paneling – had trundled into the alleyway and came to a stop behind Sadé's two-story clapboard home. All the lights in the house were on. Surrounded by a waist-high chainlink fence that was warped and bowed inward in places, the backyard was a desolate graveyard of broken Nerf guns, flat and abandoned bicycle tires, and a number of sadly deflated footballs and basketballs.

"Just me and Shell," Prinny said and stepped out of the first sprinter with her red leather Hermés Birkin bag open and he butt of her 10-millimeter Glock sticking up out of it.

There were six comfortable black leather seats in the rear passenger compartment of the Sprinter van. Aqua, Asia and Thick Doll were listening as Kimmy Kakes told them about how nervous she'd been during her first comedy gig at Lynn's Laugh Lounge in Bronzeville. Aqua and Thick Doll had been there. So had Blicky Nicky, Cherish Taylor, Bunny XXX, Shmoney Rose, and Prinny. An MTN camera crew had filmed the entire event, though mostly only Kimmy's set would be shown in episode five of *The Real Baddies of Chicago* when Season Three aired in March.

"We shouldn't be here, Prinny," Shell complained bitterly as she stepped down from inside the van and closed the sliding door behind her. She had a certain look in her eyes that Prinny perceived to be a hybrid mixture of fear and regret. She chewed at the corner of her bottom lip and flicked her eyes left, right, front back, all around "We should just go to the club and enjoy our night. We can FaceTime Sadé in the morning and talk this out."

Prinny ignored the suggestion, thinking *Yeah, that's a great idea. Give her all the time she needs to contact the police ad implicate me in a fucking murder.* She looked at Zoodie and tipped her head to the side, motioning for him to follow her. He came around from behind L-Stone and the gang and crossed the rocky alley way to join Prinny and Shell at the closed, leaning chainlink gate in Sadé's backyard fence. To the tight was a grimy yellow clapboard garage with a big blue six-pointed star spraypainted on the side Two raised pitchforks rose behind the star in a X-like formation, the tines pointed toward the wet, dripping roof. The letters G.D.N. were spayed above the star, initials that even a street gang novice knew stood for Gangster Disciple Nation.

"Y'all get back in the van," Prinny said to L-Stone and the gang. "I don't want anybody riding past and seeing y'all standin' out here with them guns. I'll be good in here I got Zoodie, and you know I got my blick on me."

L-Stone nodded once and thumped a fist off his chest. *Stone Love.* He ducked his narrow, peanut brown head and climbed back into the Sprinter. His hair was done in shoulder-length dreadlocks, just like Keymon's and Braylon's. Monk was the only one with a shaved scalp. He was also the only one with a Glock; the others toted Dracos.

Prinny had to lift the gate on it's rusted hinges to get it open. She entered the yard with her eyes on the glowing yellow squares of light in the back of the house. The noisy cacophony of wild young children came from those windows. Shrieking laughter and high pitched squeals of joy.

Two houses down, a backyard festivity of some sort was taking place. Drunken voices and laugher of the young adult variety, some of them singing along to Ginuwine's "Stingy" as it throbbed from their sound system. There was a lot more love in the Windy City than there was hatred, regardless of what the news media and drill rap might lead people to believed. That backyard kickback was only exhibit A.

"That van is *nice* on the inside," Zoodie commented from close behind Prinny. The concrete walkway leading to Sadé's back steps was cracked in dozens of places. Cold resistant weeds sprouted from the cracks to caress and console the broken toys and airless rubber that shared the walkway with them. "I swear," Zoodie said, "it was like being on a private jet sittin' back there. The champagne buckets. That great big TV. Those thick leather seats. Man, That's living."

"What did y'all do," Prinny asked jokingly, "bond over your mutual love of deadlocks?"

The joke elicited two drab chuckes from Zoodie, "Haha. Very funny." He didn't sound very amused.

They climbed the three wooden steps to Sadé's back porch. The stairs were soft and spongy underfoot. The trio of visitors triggered a proximity sensor in the light above the door and it came on in a blinding flash of white that was at least a thousand watts more poweful than the jaundiced yellow glow of the windows.

"Jesus Christ," Prinny said, though she considered herself a Muslim. She visored her hand over her eyes and clenched her teeth, mad at a lightbulb.

Shell went to open the screen exterior door and struggled on the pull; the lower half of the door didn't agree with being separated from its frame. It finally came open with a wobbling clang just as the cream-colored inner door swung inward, and standing there with one hand on the side of the door and the other holding a half-gallon bottle of Hennessy was Sadé Dobbs.

Clad in a dark blue University of Chicago sweater over sky blue jeans with darker blue veins traversing the denim fabric and blue and white Jordan sneakers, Sadé looked a whole lot better than Prinny had expected. She wore an auburn-colored wig that fell down past her shoulders at a neatly shorn angle. Her skin complexion was what you would get if you microwaved a couple of milk chocolate Hershey's bars and poured the resulting liquid over the head of a mannequin. Her eyes were the color of wet baby shit and her smile was hale and healthy.

"What the hell y'all doing here?" Sadé moved aside so they could enter her small, well-arranged kitchen. The linoleum was rotten and discolored around the edges, and the lower part of the walls were an artwork of childish scribbling and small handprints -- clear evidence of the six mini terrorists to whom Sadé had given birth –but the rest of the kitchen was put together pretty well.

Looking at Sadé, the first image that came to Prinny's mind was the fat white woman dancing in the street in that grotesquely happy Wegovy commercial. Sadé was a thick girl, always had been, but she'd lost a shitload of weight since the last time Prinny had seen her. Prinny figured the dramatic weight loss had come as a direct result of one of those monthly GLP-1 injections. Wegovy, Ozempic, Mounjaro, Zepbound; one of those.

The next image that came to Prinny was a cheese nibbling rat in an auburn wig and a blue University of Chicago sweater.

She put on a perfect facsimile of a smile and sat down at a table that was small and square and hewn from ash wood. She got a text from Cynthia Campbell – an MTN field producer who was called Sin City not only because it completed her first name but also because Las Vegas was her hometown – regarding tonight's filming at QOD and spent a thoughtful moment replying to that while Nishelle introduced Zoodie to Sadé and vice versa. Shell's introduction labeled Zoodie as Prinny's boyfriend, which compelled Sadé to regard the two of them with a sly smirk.

"Okay, sis ," Sadé said, and gave Prinny a light pound on the shoulder. "I remember you tellin' me about him when you and Aqua got back from Miami that time. Aqua showed me a video of him dancing for some girls at a bachelorette party."

"Where is *your* boyfriend?" Prinny looked up from her phone. She watched Sadé's eyes go from sly to nervous as they darted over to Shell and back. "Because we need to have a talk. A serious talk And you know exactly what it's about too, so don't play stupid."

Sadé's lips and eyelids moved slowly away from each other, widening at a rate of about an inch per second, until her eyes were like silver dollars with shit brown irises drawn in the middle of them and her mouth gaped wide enough to show all five of her cavities. She set her bottle down on the Formica counter and turned to Nishelle.

"You told her," she said accusingly.

"I couldn't *not* tell her," Shell retorted. "The fuck? You call me with some weird shit like that and expect me to keep it to myself? This one of my best friends. One of *our* best friends. The fuck?"

"Where is your boyfriend?" Prinny repeated, more firmly than before. She felt an infernal heat rising inside her, as if a dark miracle of alchemy had taken all the food and drinks she'd ingested throughout the day and combined them to create a well of molten gold.

Meanwhile, the look on Sadé's pie-shaped face suggested that the contents of her stomach had turned to stone. If her asshole was square she might have shit bricks. "He..He went to go pick up our sandwiches from Potbelly, and to grab some cigarettes. We, uhh.." She looked at her big bottle of Hennessy. " Some people down the street invited us to this backyard Valentine's party. It's supposed to be like an R&B thing, for grown folks. I paid my neighbor's daughter to come over and watch the kids. Tramell's supposed to be meeting me at the party He should be pullin' up any minute."

Sadé's tone of voice was low and defeated. She took to a chair across the table from Prinny and sat with her head slumped forward, wagging it from side to side and sighing again and again. She picked at fingernails that weren't even there, as they were all chewed down nearly to the cuticles. From somewhere upstairs came a loud thump, followed by a squall of prepubescent laughter. Sadé raised her subdued gaze to the ceiling, opened her mouth and sucked in a breath to shout, then reconsidered and dropped her head again.

"I be high man," she confessed. "Tweakin'. Tramell got me smokin' that bullshit gas station weed he be gettin' from them Arabs" She pronounced it *Ay-rabs*. "They call it Tunechi. Sometimes it gives you like a good weed high, but sometimes..." she exhaled an emphatic whoosh of air. "...man, sometimes that shit *fucks you up*. Like, for real for real. Have you thinkin' all kinda crazy shit. Just the other day I took two lil hits off a blunt Tramell and Pine-Sol was smokin' and the next thing I know I'm standin' butt-naked in the washing machine, tryna get my big ass down in there and hide from the devil in the ice cream truck."

Zoodie had started laughing when Sadé mentioned the man whose nickname was Pine-Sol and now there were tears in his eyes and he was holding his belly in both of his strong black hands. He bent over and slapped his knee, his thick black dreads bobbling buoyantly as he did it. Nishelle was also able to see the humor in the story, rummaging up a chuckle and a smirk as she planted her hands on her hips an set in on her relative.

"Listen, cousin: if you smokin' some shit that got you wantin' to snitch on somebody, then bitch you need to find some'n else to smoke. Try a Newport. A Black and Mild. Hell, a crack pipe! I know a hundred and one crackheads, and ain't naan one of em ever tried to hide in a washing machine thinkin' a devil in an ice cream truck was comin' after em." Nishelle sucked her teeth. "I hope the kids didn't see you like that."

Sadé lowered her head another couple of inches and shook it from right to left, a genuine show of embarrassment.

"Romaniquana came in there and found me."

Zoodie stifled another laugh— or at least he tried to. It came out of him anyway, like a newborn baby forcing its way into the world after nine long months of gestation. He turned to face the wall behind him and pressed his forehead against it, clutching at his abdomen and laughing like a maniac.

Prinny had joked with the other girls in her crew about the absurd names Sadé had given her children so many times in the past that she was all snickered out, but still she issued a resonant growl from deep in her throat and said, "Please stop callin' her that."

"Why?" Sadé sat up straight. "It's her name."

"Did Tramell try to talk you into getting me arrested?" Prinny asked to shift the topic of conversation back to the much more important subject.

Sadé nodded. "Kinda sorta." Fresh tears welled up and danced atop her lower eyelids. She sniffled. "We was high on that shit and got to talkin' about what had just happened to Baby Slim, 'bout how his dirty ass stepdaddy broke his nose and his ribs and all that, and that's when I told Tramell about the night Gutterville Slim got killed."

A sour grimace passed across Prinny's lovely brown features. She opened her mouth to speak her mind, to ask Sadé why she would go and do some dumb shit like that, but they had been friends for so long that Sadé could practically read her thoughts.

"I know, Prinny. Why would I tell him about *that*, right? Well, like I just told y'all I was high, and thinkin' about it when I was high got me to talkin' about it with Tramell. He got all paranoid about it, talm 'bout he had seen some Tubi movie supposedly based on a true story about a girl who went to prison for life over the same kinda shit. And that shit made *me* all paranoid. I got to thinkin' the FBI was watchin' my house, listenin' in on my phone calls. And Tramell didn't make it no better when he found out they got a twelve-thousand-dollar reward for any information that can get Slim's killer locked up."

"So he wanted you to snitch on the gang for twelve racks," Prinny said with a snappy note of finality lacing her tone. " and *you* was gon' do it."

"*I was high!*" Sadé cried, and now those dancing tears went moonwalking down her cheeks. "He had me thinkin' all kinda shit! That I could go to jail for the rest of my life. That I could lose my kids. When all the kids got sick with the flu a few weeks ago, he said that was God punishing me for not doin' the right thing from day one when I accepted that money. He said that God was offerin' me that twelve thousand dollar reward so He could forgive me of my sins."

"I cain't'," Nishelle said, meaning she couldn't take any more of her cousin's insanity. She shoved open the screened door and went storming out onto the back porch, shaking her head incredulously.

Prinny stood up from her chair and dug way down in her purse to the three packets of hundred dollar bills she had piled at the very bottom. Her Glock pistol pressed into her forearm as she reached past it, and she briefly considered dragging it out and aiming it at Sadé's tear-streaked face. But what good would that do?

"Here." She slid a packet of hundreds across the table. "Ten grand. The next time you need some money, just call me and ask. And stop smokin' that Chinese chemical bullshit before you end up in a mental hospital somewhere."

"I'm done. I swear, Prinny. I swear on all my babies."

She rushed around the table and lassoed Princess in a noose of a hug that lasted an uncomfortable length of time.

There came another vicious thump from the floor above, and Prinny was leaving out the door with Zoodie right behind her, she head Sadé yell, "Zarmonico, I know that's you! Sit the *fuck* down up there!.."

Chuckling aloud, Zoodie slipped one mammoth arm around his lady's waist just as they made it to the middle of the small square yard. Prinny turned around to face him. His eyes were wet around the edges from laughing and the broad smile on his mouth betrayed his urge to laugh some more.

"I know that was a serious conversation," he said, moving his hands down her back to rub and knead the fleshy protuberances just below her waist, "but man, that was one of the funniest conversations I ever heard in my life. Devil in a ice cream truck? Sounds like a Quentin Tarrantino movie. And what's with those *names*?"

"That bitch is crazy," Prinny reasoned. She reached up to thumb the moisture from around his eyes. An easterly gust of wind blew through the yard, slightly rearranging the heavy dreadlocks that framed his irresistibly handsome face.

"What was that about Gutterville Slim? Ain't he one of the boys you shot in self-defense a few years back?"

"No, but they were Gutterville Mickey Cobras too. Their names were MCG and Snake."

"So you've killed *three* people."

"No!" Prinny's head jerked back on her neck. Her eyes became cold and accusatory beneath the furrowed shelf of her brow. "Look, I ain't killed nobody, okay? You can't say that kinda shit. Rumor like those get niggas killed in Chicago. Don't ever say that again."

Zoodie capitulated, raising his hands as if she'd pulled her gun on him. A part of Prinny wanted to regret snapping at him like that, but a greater part of her viewed it as a necessary evil. Some things just had to be said.

"A'ight," he said. "My bad." He chuckled once. "Just tryna get it all together in my head, that's all. Trust me, if I had loose lips, half the street niggas in Miami would be in

76

prison. I'm a real nigga, baby. I might not be in the streets like my brothers, I might be a stripper and all that, but I'm still a real nigga."

Prinny sighed through her nose and pressed the side of her head against the stone all of his chest. "I know," she murmured. "It's just that… you know… I've got too much on the line. Too much to lose. One wrong move and my empire crumbles. I can't let that happen."

"If that's the case, you might need to get somebody to silence Sadé's boyfriend. Seems to me like he's the real problem. And don't get L-Stone or any of his boys to do it, because that might tie back to you."

" I know who to call."

She peeled away from Zoodie's embrace and drew in a deep tremulous breath. As she and Zoodie headed back out into the alleyway, she thumbed her way down the list of contacts in her iPhone until she got to the names that began with the thirteenth letter of the English alphabet. The letter M.

Millionaire Markio.

Just looking at his name gave her the stomach flu. It was as if a fissure had opened in the lining of her lower intestine and billowed out a hot, sickening volcanic steam. She could not bear calling him—the idea of speaking with him, of actually hearing his voice, was way more nauseating than the mere sight of his name—so she composed a simple four word text an sent it before she lost her nerve.

So lost was Prinny in her thoughts about the man she'd just texted that she hardly even felt it when Zoodie eased his arms around her from behind, For a long moment she simply stood there next to her Sprinter van, hearing Chris Brown's "Residuals" playing at the backyard fiesta two houses down and a G-Harbo song playing inside the Sprinter without really hearing either of them. Her Mexican driver/bodyguard, Jesus Godinez, stood waiting a few feet ahead of her with his hand on the handle of the side sling door, and though he wore an all-white designer business suit that was impossible to miss, Princess barely even noticed him.

She was experiencing a flashback of the night she'd walked into the doorway of her ex-boyfriend's home office and found him sitting behind his desk with her half-sister, Kamari, planted on his lap.

It was the pleasurable feel of Zoodie's lips coming to rest on the nape of her neck that brought Prinny back to the present.

"You okay, baby?" Zoodie asked.

Prinny nodded and slipped her phone into her purse.

"What are you thinking about?"

"I just texted somebody I really had no plan of contacting again."

"To help you with the Tramell situation?

"Yeah." She treated the side of her forehead to a light, absentminded scratching.

"Who was it, Markio?"

She nodded her head.

"If you need his help to keep that dopefiend from ruining you, then get his help. I don't like him either, you know. Voltaire Muck was the head guy for the Zoes in Miami. His brother, Keondre, was the highest paid running back in the NFL. They took care of all the kids in Little Haiti, bought them backpacks full of school supplies, turkeys for Thanksgiving and toys for Christmas— the whole nine."

Prinny knew the rest of the story – Millionaire Markio had supposedly owed more than two million dollars to his ex, Whitney Clarrett, and she began dating Voltaire Muck, he'd gone after Markio for the money, only to end up shot dead in a grisly quadruple murder that was rumored to have been orchestrated by Markio himself – but Zoodie didn't get a chance to say any of that, because at that exact moment Thick Doll raked open the sliding door and stuck her scowling face out at Princess.

"Girl, if you don't come on!" Thick Doll exclaimed, and left the threat unfinished.

Prinny smiled and turned to peck Zoodie on the lips, pressing the palms of her comparably small hands against his rock-solid slabs of pectoral muscles as she did it. Then she climbed into the Sprinter and endured a round of abusive rhetoric from the close-knit group of young black women as she often referred to as her bitches, while Jesus drove them to Queen of Diamonds.

Chapter 9

We need to talk.

Markio Earl read the text message only once, but it remained on his mind for a long while after, flashing on and off like the broad blue neon sign that read Queen of Diamonds in bold script. The sign shone from atop a pole that rose from the corner of the strip club's roof. He could see it from where he sat in the backseat of his pearly white Rolls Royce Cullinan, though he only glanced up at it once as Apple, his friend of over thirty years, drove his $600,000 SUV into the vast parking lot behind the fairly opulent gentlemen's club.

Four more Rolls Royce's shadowed them into the parking lot; another Cullinan and three Phantom's, each one as bone-white as the one Millionaire Markio rode in.

"You's a bold nigga," Apple said, stretching out the word *bold* for two full seconds. "I'll give you that. 'Cause ain't no way in hell I'd be showin' up here."

"Yeah?" Marko looked up from his Kindle computer tablet. He was reading *If You Cross Me Once*, an Anthony Fields novel, for inspirational purposes, as he'd been experiencing a bout of writer's block over the past couple of weeks. He set the tablet down on the vacant seat next to him to offer the fat man his undivided attention. "Why not?"

"Because the same man who aimed his rifle into your garage from a hundred yards away and blew Lil Archie's brains out, thinkin' he was you, is the same old man who left seven dead bodies in this parkin' lot. *That's* why not?"

"He left *six* dead bodies in the parking lot," Markio corrected his friend. "The seventh body got left in a trash can in that alley back there."

"Same fuckin' difference! That old man tried to *kill* you. He killed Lil Archie because he thought Archie was *you*. And look at what he did to Weezy. Blew up his car while he was sittin' in it, and that was *after* he came out here and laid down seven of Weezy's guys, right outside of this strip club."

"Shit happens." Markio hitched his shoulders.

"Shit happens?" Apple tried twisting his blubbering brown body in his seat to look back at the man who paid all his bill, reconsidered, and adjusted the rearview mirror to glower at Markio's reflection. "Shit *happens*! That old muthafucka tried to take yo' head off wit' a goddam sniper rifle! What if he ducked off in this parkin' lot right now, waitin' on you to show up so he can finally getcho stupid ass? What if he walk up right when I park this muhfucka and shoot you right through the window?"

"You worry too much," Markio said. He curled his first two fingers and wrapped the middle knuckles against this window. "See? Bulletproof glass."

"Don't get me shot, nigga. I already got shot up once, fuckin' around with Rell and Jahlil. I ain't' tryna lose my life, get shot from twenty or thirty yards away by some military sniper, all 'cause you wanna pop out and show niggas how tough you is."

"Herb is dead somewhere. You worried about a dead man."

"Cain't be too dead, FBI got him on their most wanted list. Ain't no way in hell they're offerin' eight million dollars for a dead man."

Markio gave another shrug, picked up his double-stacked Styrofoam cups from the cupholder, and took a generous swallow of Lean. He'd mixed the narcotic brew himself. Four carefully measured ounces of Wockhardt promethazine and codeine syrup, pineapple-flavored Fanta soda, and five squared cubes of ice. He'd developed a taste for the drink shortly after stumbling upon a heroin kingpin's cash savings at a storage auction a few years ago, and he'd been hooked on it ever since.

He gazed out his window as Apple maneuvered the bulky SUV into one of the yellow-lined RESERVED PARKING slots near the club's rear entrance. A sloping concrete walkway flanked by dark blue-painted steel railings ran sideways from the blue steel door to the parking lot. The two big men standing outside the door wee dark in hue and twinning in identical black skullcaps, peacoats, leather gloves, slacks, and dress shoes that were so black and shiny they could have been hewn from the skin of a baby seal.

"You think Princess gon' be here tonight?" Apple asked.

"Shit, I don't know. She might be. She texted me a few minutes ago sayin' we need to talk."

Markio grinned at the idea of Prinny needing to speak with him after all the mean-spirited words she'd sent his way via social media and her star-studded podcast, *Prinny Said What?* There had even been an episode of *The Real Baddies* that showed all the girls coming together in a rare show of love and support to embrace Prinny the morning after she caught Markio with her sister on his lap. A great number of her followers had come after him following the airing of that episode. He had disabled the comments on his Instagram page an uninstalled all the social media apps from both of his iPhones, but the trolls had persisted, giving his novels one-star ratings on Amazon and leaving blistering reviews that had nothing to do with the book in question and everything to do with him being a backstabbing cheater.

He raised himself up to reach over the back of his seat to the rear storage area and grab his large white leather Louis Vuitton duffle bag. Piled neatly inside it were fifty packets of hundred dollars bills. Five hundred thousand dollars. Resting on the surface of the cash were two .40 caliber Glock

27 Gen 5 pistols and a Century Arms Micro Draco 7.62-millimeter assault pistol.

In his experience, guns were a necessity for a man who had money. The two went together like bread and butter.

The parking lot was almost completely full. From one side to the other people were climbing out of cars and trucks and walking toward the front of the club to join the line of paying patrons. Markio had been assured by the top boss of Mexico's reigning drug cartel that Herbert Harris, the eighty-something-year-old Vietnam war veteran who'd killed Weezy and attempted to kill Markio himself, would no longer be a problem. Yet and still, he found himself studying the men who crossed the parking lot on foot, looking for a bowlegged elder, with coal black skin and a lightly stooped geriatric gait.

He didn't find an old man, but he did see the black G-Wagon pull into a reserved parking space a few slots over. He knew that his boy Two Ton's girlfriend, Jaresha, had a truck that looked just like it, so he was not surprised to see her climb down from inside it. What surprised him was that she headed straight for his Cullinan, not going around his motley clan of fellow gang members as they exited the other four Rolls-Royces but walking straight through them. Her strides were so strong and purposeful that she might have walked right through a brick house if it got in her way, like maybe she and the Kool-Aid man shared the same father.

He pushed open his door and was moving his legs to get out when Jaresha walked up and stopped right in front of him, blocking his way.

"We need to talk," she said, placing one hand on her thickly rounded hip.

Markio chuckled once. "What the fuck is that, the quote of the day or some'n?" He spoke to her in his friendliest tone of voice, not only because she was so incredibly attractive and he'd harbored a secret crush on her for years but also because she was the kind of woman who demanded respect.

She squinted her eyes and furrowed her brow in confusion, then her hard expression returned and she said, "I just got robbed behind The Visionary Lounge. Bitch-ass niggas took my watch, my diamond AP. They would've got my chain if YoungNya and her people hadn't walked out when they did."

"Who was it?"

"Some niggas named Rock and his sister Nay's baby daddy. How do I know that? Because the dumbass baby daddy, who wasn't even smart enough to wear a mask, kept referring to the dude as Rock and Rock got mad at him about it. They was about to shoot each other."

Markio knew of four men on the west side of Chicago who went by the name Rock. One of them was wheelchair-bound. Another was an enforcer for the Black Souls street gang, but he didn't have any sisters, and he'd lived on 16th Street and Christian Ave for most of his life, which was just up the way from Jaresha's Millard Avenue home. She would have recognized him.

The other two Rocks were Rodrick McDuffy and Delmar Robinson. Both of themwere, like Markio, longtime members of the Traveling Vice Lords. Roderick was a ranking member of the Cali Boy faction of TVLs, a big dog who owned properties and presided over a large-cale heroin operation that was fueled by the drug shipments Markio received from the Matamoros Cartel. Delmar represented the Wicked Town TVL faction. Markio had only met him in passing, at the annual TVL picnic that was held at Garfield Perk last year.

"What did Rock look like?" Markio asked.

"Tall. Maybe like six-one, six-two?" Jaresha's shoulders jumped, and her eyes assumed a vacant, lackluster expression as she thought back to the robbery. "Skinny. He had on a mask, and you could tell he was clean. His partner was the total opposite." Her pretty face morphed into a disgusted sneer. "He had dreads, dirty dreads with spots of lint all through them, and his *breath* … Oh my *GOD*."

Markio started laughing. So did his cousins Kay and Buck, both of whom had swaggered over to stand beside Jaresha as she was busy describing the men who'd robbed her. Within the next couple of seconds all the passengers from the other four Rolls-Royces migrated toward the open rear drivers' side door of Markio's Cullinan. They were all dressed like him in high-end designer gear and diamond jewelry. Markio wore a Chrome Hearts ensemble that consisted of a cotton sweater and pants that faded from white to gray to black. His skull cap was a matching ski-mask he wore rolled up to his forehead. Around his neck hung a bevy of Cuban-link necklaces and tennis chains that were replete with VVS quality white diamonds. The pendants hanging from the Cuban-links had white diamond incrustations, and two of them spelled out MILLIONAIRE MARKIO and FREE LORD N'EM. The third pendant was an iced-out Chicago Bears logo. His Patek Philippe wristwatch had cost him $319,000 and was made almost entirely of interconnecting baguette diamonds.

He climbed down from inside his luxury SUV, handed his duffle bag off to Apple when the fat man joined him a moment later, and told Jaresha he'd do all he could to recover her stolen watch. And then, to reassure her, he had all his people produce their phones and put out the word via text that he had ten thousand dollars for the return of Kitty Jae's stolen watch.

"I wanna know who set it up too," she said, folding her arms across her chest. "I swear to God, if it was..." She trailed off, flaring her nostrils, clenching her teeth, and shaking her beautiful head. She took a moment to recompose herself. "Get my shit back," she said and walked back to her G-Wagon.

Markio and his boys ogled her meaty derriere as she went. Most of them had girlfriends and wives at home, but they stared like they didn't. They stared the way small children stare at gift-wrapped boxes beneath the tree at Christmastime, the way A$AP Rocky probably gawked at Rihanna's jaw-dropping curves whenever she came sauntering in the bedroom wet and dripping from the shower. Their hungrily blatant stares were accompanied by an exhilarating round of catcalls:

"Just imagine hittin' that from the back."

"Two Ton don't know what to do wit' all dat! You might as well let a real nigga get in where he fit in!"

"*Damn*, Jaresha! I'll drink yo' dirty bath water through a straw! You hear me?"

"Lil mama bad as hell, on bro."

None of the comments came from Markio, though he was in agreement with most of them. He stared after Jaresha until she disappeared from view. Then sipping at his drink, he texted Big Gabby to let her know he was outside waiting for her to let him and his gang in through the back.

He was almost finished with the text message when the rubbery sounds of tire treads on wet asphalt made him look up from his phone.

In perfect military formation, seven snow white Cadillac Escalades came slicing into the parking lot. They were the larger ESV models. Four black Mercedes Sprinter vans came in behind them. Two of the Escalades broke off from the pack and began zipping in and out of the rows of parked vehicles, while the others found parking in the reserved section.

"That gotta be Alexus and her people," Apple said, tearing open the wrapper on a double-stuffed oatmeal cream pie he'd taken from his jacket pocket.

Just then, the big blue back door on the backside of Queen of Diamonds burst open, and Big Gabby sashayed out onto the walkway with her flabby brown arms thrown wide in welcome. She looked like an overweight mermaid in her tight green dress. Her smile was as wide as her hips.

Markio started off toward her wearing a broad smile of his own, his every step marked by the light metallic ching of his necklaces clashing about his neck. His main reason for coming to the strip club to begin with was to support Big Gabby. He'd known her for close to thirty years, and she was one of the select few friends he had whose love and loyalty had only strengthened over time.

Big Gabby was tall for a woman; she was five-eleven without heels, and she always were heels. Markio, on the other hand, was a hair under five and half feet tall. She closed her arms around him and for a long, heavenly moment he was lost in three hundred pounds of warmth. When she finally pulled back, she held him by the shoulders and looked him up and down.

"Boy, you lookin' good," she said, showing all her teeth.

"Thank you. That's a nice dress you got on."

"I mean, I try," Her smile burgeoned to show that her gums were as healthy as her teeth. "I knew you would come. Didn't think that bitch would come," she said, pointing to where the two white Escalades were parked. "but I know I could count on you."

"You can always count on me. I show up for all my niggas."

"Don't start no shit in my VIP Lounge, I know y'all got guns and all that, but don't let me see them on camera."

Markio nodded and sipped his Lean. On the side of the outer cup he'd scrawled *Free Cocky Lord* in gold, glittery ink.

"Go on in," Gabby said, and moved past him to hug Apple. "My assistant will lead the way. Let me welcome Alexus and Prinny, and then I'll be right up."

Markio hadn't realized that there was someone standing behind Big Gabby until she moved past him. The girl was long and wiry, though not as tall as her boss. Her scrawny bare shoulders were raised against the chilly night air, and it took Markio a couple of looks to realize that her skinny legs weren't naked like her shoulders The leggings she wore under her gray and white minidress were the same sepia hue as her skin.

"Hey." She smiled with her eyes and smirked with her lips. "I'm Jayda, Gabby's personal assistant. Big fan of your books. Come follow me."

Markio squinted at her back as she led him and his noisy entourage into a wide, brightly lit corridor. The floor was made up of gray marble tiles and there were three doors on each side of the hallway, each one spaced far away from the other. The first door on the left opened into a large rectangular room with granite tables running along two walls and widescreen TV monitors suspended from the ceiling so that the two or three security personnel on camera duty could observe themselves and the rest of the club from over four dozen cameras that were mounted both inside and outside of the building. The room beside it was Big Gabby's office, and the third door opened into the health and fitness spa where a lot of the girls went to exercise and relax when they weren't on the clock.

The first door on the right was the tip-out room – the dancers went there to pay whatever tips they owed to the DJ, the VIP Host, and the House Mom before going home – and the third door was a utility closet where all the toiletries and cleaning supplied were stored, but it was the middle door that Markio was hoping to look into. That was the Prime Shift locker room. Sadly though, that door was shut.

"Damn," Markio said to the closed door.

"We got two bouncers in there to keep Blicky Nicky's nutty ass from swingin' on Shmoney Rose," Jayda said as they passed the door. She had her arms crossed over her flat chest like a native of Wakanda, and she was using her hands to rub the heat back into her knobby brown shoulders. "That girl is scary. I went in there to check on her a lil while ago, and she swung on me! Like, literally tried to punch me in the face. She lucky I'm on probation."

"Have we met before?" Markio asked as they were approaching the door at the far end of the hallway, which opened into the stairwell. "You look familiar."

Jayda looked back at him, smiling with her eyes. Tyra Banks might have called that *smizing*.

"You dated my auntie," said the skinny woman-child. "She and I do look alike. That might be it. Or you might have seen me on her TikTok. I'm the one who's always pranking her."

"And her name is...?"

"Oh shit," she chortled. "That's my bad. That is totally my bad. I call her Auntie Yazzy, but you probably know her as Bunny."

"Oh yeah, Bunny." Markio grinned at a thousand good memories, and suddenly he remembered where he'd seen the cutely bespectacled teen. There had been a glass cube of family photos on Bunny's coffee table. She'd explained that the cheerleader in the photos was Jayda, her sixteen-year-old niece. That was two years ago. "Yeah, that's where I saw you. In that glass square of pictures she kept on that table. What are you, eighteen now?"

"Uhh-huh. August twentieth I'll be nineteen. Auntie still got that cube on her table too. I moved it the other day, and she 'bout bit my head off."

"She here tonight?"

"Mm-hm. Just pulled in before you did. That's her green and white Maserati truck parked a few spaces over from your Rolls Royce." She paused as they entered the stairwell and smized over her shoulder at him. "Gabby's always watching the camera. We watched you pull in."

"Her police ass," Markio said, and *police* came out as *po-leece*, not because he was miseducated but because he preferred the saucier vernacular of his cultural upbringings.

The quip elicited a sweet giggle from his teenage usher.

Inside the stairwell, the walls were baby blue, the stairs had dark blue carpeting, and the air smelled faintly of paint.

The cinderblock walls muffled the instrumental record of Twista's "Overdose" but the vocals of the rap legend's live performance came through loud and clear.

Markio took out his cell phone and reread Prinny's text as he climbed the stairs. *We need to talk.* What the hell did that mean? Surely, she didn't need his help the way Jaresha did; L-Stone and the rest of the Moes she'd grown up around were just as deeply rooted into the streets of Chicago as Markio and his Dark Side Fraction of Traveling Vice Lords. On top of that Princess was a successful businesswoman, the creator of one of television's most beloved reality shows. The money it would cost her to neutralize a threat was a raindrop to the ocean of her net worth.

There were two doors on the second floor landing. The one on the right led down a long, blue carpeted hallway where all private rooms were located. Jayda led the way into the door on the left which opened in the rear of the VIP Lounge.

A dozen sights, sounds, and smells hit Markio all at once. The air was redolent of exotic weed smoke. Twista's rapid-fire lyrics and the beat they rode were much louder and intelligible here than in the stairwell. Seven or eight Preferred Shift dancers bounced their fat jiggly asses and wiggled their meaty brown thighs near the VIP tables, while dollar bills swooped and spun through the air around them. Among the famous faces in the section were Malachi "Fly Guy" Mitchell, a power forward for the Chicago Bulls; Lee "Juice" Wilkins, a former drug kingpin and high ranking TVL from Markio's neighborhood who'd made it out of the game with a sterling reputation and a rumored nine-figure nest egg to boot; Juice's wife Lakita "Bubbles" Wilkins, who'd gone from being a stripper and Hip-Hop music video vixen to a real estate tycoon and perhaps most notably, a renowned painter with two of her canvases gracing the walls at the iconic Metropolitan Museum of Art; Johnna Broward, the billionaire CEO of Panteon Technologies whose net worth of $34 billion made her the second-richest black woman in the world behind Alexus Costilla-King. Johnna's date was Bartholomew Jones, the lead actor in 4Nem, a TV series Markio had recently written and executive produced for MTN.

Dawn and Shawnna, Juices' immensely gorgeous identical twin daughters, had snagged the gig as tonight's VIP hosts. Apple handed one of them (Markio could never tell the twins apart, though he knew that Shawnna was married to his younger cousin Bankroll Reese) three packets of hundred dollar bills to exchange for thirty grand in singles.

Markio's table was at the very front of the VIP lounge, between Juice's table and a vacant one. The back of the sofa rested against a glass wall that overlooked the main floor below. Markio looked back and spent a long moment admiring all the people, the great majority of whom were rocking along to the rap performance. Two strippers had climbed high up on one of the poles, almost to the ceiling; a lot of folks were watching them too. The bar was far away from the elevated dais that Twista and his hype man were performing on, but there was an enormous television back there that showed the performance in high definition.

"This bitch *lit*, gang!" Apple shouted, ripping open another cream pie. "On bro! Look at all dese hoes. Look at that ho over there. She just did the splits on that nigga *lap*! I'm tryna find out *her* name."

Markio looked at the stripper Apple was ogling and put on a smile that felt as fake as the silicone in the exotic dancer's chest. No matter how hard he tried to become lost in the moment, he simply could not stop thinking about Prinny's text message. What did it mean? Did she need his help in dealing with something in the streets, the way Jaresha needed him to track down her stolen watch? Or maybe she missed him as much as he missed her and had decided to forgive him for fucking her sister half a hundred times Maybe she wanted to give him another chance.

The mere consideration of the latter possibility filled his lungs with a hopeful breath.

He checked the time on his phone and saw that it was 9:43 p.m. Seventeen minutes until Prime Shift's steatopygic beauties came in and turned things up a notch. He figured Princess was probably downstairs in the Prime Shift locker room, maybe giving the girls from her reality show a motivational pep talk, maybe filming a quick segment for the show.

Whatever she was doing, Markio couldn't wait to see her.

It wasn't that Markio Earl was lacking in the way of female companionship. He was a critically-acclaimed urban fiction novelist and an Oscar nominated screenwriter. He'd accumulated somewhere around forty-three million dollars off his books, movies, and the two prime time thrillers that had recently debuted on MTN, and there was a lot more rolling in. Women were like bloodhounds when it came to sniffing out a man's success, and their seasoned snouts had guided hundreds of thousands of them right to Millionaire Mariko's digital doorstep. He had over five million followers on Instagram and two million more on X. His reputation for showering his women with lavish gifts came from his three-year-old son's mother, Mya Patterson, and Prinny sharing videos of their cars, jewelry and wardrobes with all their followers and tagging him in the thank you posts. The unintended result of that exposure had sent a massive herd of baddies stampeding into his direct messages, many of them just as famous as Princess Kelly and her supermodel half-sister Kamari White.

That being said, finding a woman hadn't been a problem for Markio in quite a while. What he was looking for now was the *right* woman, a woman whose goals and dreams ran parallel to his; a woman he could trust to keep her lips sealed when it came to his implicit dealings with the Matamoros drug cartel, and his vicarious overseeing of one of the most powerful street gangs in Chicago history.

Princess Kelly checked all the boxes.

Markio stood to shake Juice's hand and pound the big man's shoulder. Then he gave Bubbles a one-armed embrace and returned to his seat. There he sat sipping his lean and taking it all in while his gang, many of them with their own Styrofoam cups in hand, settled in all around him.

Every man in Millionaire Markio's entourage was gangster. Their fashion choices varied, but every single one of them sported a white diamond Cuban link necklace with an iced out FBS pendant. FBS was short for Fin Ball Shortiez. The origin of the crew name was unclear—some claimed Rev, the neighborhood barber, had coined the name after witnessing a group of the rowdy young Vice Lords stomp out a pair of rivals a few blocks east of his shop, while others swore it was Markio's cousin Kay who'd christened the name—but what *was* clear was that Millionaire Markio was the leader of FBS. He'd paid good drug money for their diamond chains and watches. He bailed them out of jail when they got arrested, and when there was no bail he squandered thousands on really good lawyers to beat the case. For the members who'd graduated high school and moved on to college, Markio paid their tuition fees. And when FBS Stix, a rising drill rapper whose debut mixtape had done exceedingly well, was maimed in a New Year's Eve shooting near McKinley Park, Millionaire Markio had cleared the six-figure hospital bill, hired a fine ass Pureto Rian nurse to tend to Stix's wounds, and put out a $50,000 bounty on the head of Stix's shooter.

And so, seated amongst his brood of gangbanging misfits, with the round-bodied Apple to his right and the wolf-faced Gucci Ball to his left, Millionaire Markio felt safe and comfortable enough to sip at his drink and thumb through the latest carousel of bikini-clad photos Prinny had posted on Instagram.

The photos were taken at the Dreams Bahia Mia Surf & Spa Resort in Nayarit, Mexico. The first few pics showed Prinny with the entire cast of *The Real Baddie of Chicago*, posing between a swimming pool and a row of equidistantly spaced chaise lounges. then there was a sexy photo of Prinny reclining in one of the chaise lounges. She wore a silver and black two-piece Dior bikini that concealed little more than her nipples and labia. She was drinking something fruity through a straw while perusing a Zadie Smith paperback.

Apple leaned in to stare, "Jeezus Christ," he said, swiveling his head with each syllable. "Now that's just too thick right there. Man. God broke the mold when he made her. She 'bout thick as Sza. I fuck around and nut fo' I even get in that pussy."

Markio chuckled jauntily and was about to swipe to the next pic when Apple leaned in again.

"Speakin' of Prinny, I hope she ain't dumb enough to walk in here wit' L-Stone and them other niggas from Hyde park. It fuck around and go up."

"Aw shit," Markio said. His eyes got big, and he shot a glance to the closed stairwell door. "Nahh She wouldn't … She wouldn't do that."

"Never know." Apple hunched his shoulders. "I mean, them is her people. She grew up with them niggas, and you know they look at it like you the one got Baby Stone killed. Just sayin'. You might wanna text ya girl back and see who all she brought with her before they walk through that door."

Markio was already texting Prinny when Apple made the suggestion. He and his gang had gone to war with the Hyde Park Black P. Stones after Baby Stone, their former General, refused to pay the eight million dollars he'd owed Markio for a shipment of cocaine. Many men were shot and killed following that declaration of war, nine on Baby Stone's side and two on Mariko's. The shootings had persisted even after Baby Stone was gunned down outside his girlfriend's high end designer boutique.

In the frigid streets of Chicago, once a gang war got started, it never really came to an end. For this reason they were referred to as the Forever Wars.

The text message to Princess read: *Who you got with you??*

An urgent tap of his thumb sent the message hurdling through cyberspace. When he looked up and resettled his gaze on the stairwell door, he was no longer considering who might be coming up the stairs. His mind lingered on the distant memories of Levon "FBS Von" Ringsley and Dudley "D-Mac" McCullough, the two men from his North Lawndale neighborhood whose lives were stolen away during the war with the Black P. Stones.

He had given Von his FBS chain just two days before he was killed. The gunman had caught him walking out of the convenience store on the southeast corner of 16th Street and Drake Avenue. They'd hopped out of a white SUV with their Shiesty masks on and their guns drawn; one clumsy shooter had stumbled over his own feet and shot himself in the shoulder, but the other two opened fire on Von before he could even reach for his own pistol. He was shot nineteen times in the head; Markio paid $22,000 for Von's closed-casket funeral services.

Little Halle McCullough was just ten years old when her daddy walked her outside to get her strawberry shortcake from a passing ice cream truck on the 1600 block of South Spaulding Avenue. No one saw the shooter. A green Cadillac sedan driving by on 16th Street slowed to a crawl, and a spray of fully automatic gunfire came from an open rear passenger's side window. Both Halle and her father were shot. Halle, shot through the hand and across the top of her right ear, had survived; D-Mac, hit twice in the belly and once through the neck, had not. Two days later L-Stone had posted a video to Instagram showing him and twenty of his boys gathered in someone's basement, smoking blunts and flashing gang signs.

"We smokin' D Mac," L-Stone had said as he toked on a thick blunt. "Good D-Mac That's all we smokin' this week."

Thinking back on it now, as Markio sipped his Lean and stared fixedly at the stairwell door, he felt himself growing angrier by the second.

Chapter 10

"Why you gotta take everything I say so damn serious? It was said on the fuckin' podcast, Blicky. For entertainment."

"You know what I'ma take serious? That black eye I'ma give yo' mothafuckin ass as soon as these niggas get from between us."

Blicky tried to duck under the bouncer's thickly muscled arm, but Adonis was as fast as he was large. The veiny black arm came down like a stone pillar falling sideways and she ran right into it. The sheer force of his forearm colliding with her sternum socked all the wind from her lungs and dropped her to one knee, but she was back on her six-inch heels in an instant.

"You want some entertainment? You want some entertainment, ha? I got some entertainment for dat ass!"

She launched herself at Shmoney Rose again, but it was to no avail. Shmoney was way across the room with Cherish Taylor, Sasha the Stallion, and Bunny XXX. Even if Shmoney were to stand right behind Adonis, there was no way for Blicky to get past him. The six-five ebony giant was a part-time firefighter, employed at Englewood's Engine 54. He was accustomed to lifting fallen ceiling beams off of injured humans and throwing them aside to save the day. Holding Blicky Nicky was a cakewalk by comparison.

Kitty Jae was in no mood for the bullshit. She was at her locker when Blicky Nicky was trying to lunge past the Herculean bouncer. As soon as she was dressed – in a black lace thong and bra from Big Gabby's Whip Out lingerie line under a black fishnet bodysuit and black Louboutin heels – she spun around, took Blicky Nicky by the elbow and yanked the maniacal young woman into the restroom. There were two MTN cameramen, a field producer, and a few production assistants out in the locker room with the twenty-three other Prime Shift dancers, but the cameras weren't allowed inside the restroom.

Blicky began pacing the length of the gray marble tiled floor. "On fo'nem grave," she said, punctuating each syllable with a solid punch to the palm of her hand. "That ho got me fucked up, Kitty. She got me fucked all the way up. Talk about me on that podcast like I'm some kinda weak-ass bitch. Like I ain't from the O or some'n." She stopped packing and turned to scream at the closed restroom door. "*Bitch, I'm from Parkway Gardens! O-Block! We step on bitches like you! Sixty Fourth and King Drive, bitch! Martin Lurther King! I had a dream I knocked the teeth out of bitch mouth for talkin' about me on a podcast!*"

Fat blue veins protruded from the middle of Blicky's forehead and the sides of her neck like thick steel cables, Spittle flew from her raging mouth. She was indisputably one of the prettiest girls on Prime Shift, but the rage made her an ugly woman, if only for the moment.

"You're giving those cameramen exactly what Princess and Alexus are paying them to capture on video," Kitty Jae said, speaking calmly in hopes that her placid tone might rub off on the raving lunatic. "This is why they cast you on that show. They're exploiting you, using your anger to get viewers."

"What's the bond for murder?" Blicky replied. She had recommenced pacing the floor. The fat in her butt cheeks and boobs jiggled wildly with every furious stride. Her right hand opened and closed repeatedly as she spoke. "How much do you pay to get outta jail for killin' a ho? That's the question I need answered right now. You got your phone. Ask Siri.. Google the shit. I need to know."

'Would you really throw away your whole life over somethin' a bitch said about you on a podcast?"

"I tried sneakin' my gun in, in my purse. Big Gabby had that damned metal detector turned on, and you know that's one of those high-tech-ass Panteon cameras she got over the door. It sees right through your shit. She called me in her office and made me give it up. Fat bitch,"

Kitty Jae shook her head and sighed. She looked to her naked wrist for the time, glowered when she saw it wasn't there, and shook her head as she raised her iPhone.

The time was 9:51 p.m.

"I could shoot her in the parking lot," Blicky was saying out loud to herself. "Get my gun back from Gabby and tell her I'm going home. Sit out here in my truck and wait on them hoes to come out. I'll shoot her *and* Cherish."

Tuning out Blicky's unhinged ramblings, Kitty Jae folded her arms over her chest and leaned back against the gray plastic frame of a vacant toilet stall. All eight of the stalls were empty. A long horizontal mirror on the opposite wall spanned the length of a row of eight sink basins that had been inserted into a countertop made of the same gray marble as the floor tiles. Kitty spent a moment staring at her own reflection while thinking back on the armed robbery.

The idea that Tammy had likely set the whole thing up brought Kitty Jae's teeth together in a grinding clench and sent a whirlwind of emotion spiraling through her heart. Tears blurred her vision; she sniffed once and blinked the moisture away.

Meanwhile, Blicky Nicky continued to pace the floor, spouting the most psychotically sinister schemes her deeply disturbed brain could conjure up.

"…And you know what? That bitch is afraid of spiders. I could get my boyfriend to kidnap her, and we'll lock that ho in a box with a thousand tarantulas. I'll build the box myself. You know my daddy was a construction carpenter for a few years before he got his liquor stores. I went out on jobs with him all the time. He taught me everything he knew. I can practically build a house from the ground up, from the foundation to—"

"We got less than ten minutes," Kitty Jae interrupted. She had to interrupt Blicky because she didn't know how to stop talking on her own. "Now I don't know about you, but I'm here for the money. I got a family to feed, bills to pay, and vacations to take. I'm about to go out there and get it. I ain't comin' back to this locker room until I got at least fifty racks in my bag."

"Fifty grand?" Blicky stopped and stared at Kitty Jae. "In one night? Ain't nobody but Aqua and Cherish Taylor ever done that,"

"Fly Guy and Millionaire Markio are up there in the VIP Lounge as we speak. Fly's five-year contract with the Bulls was for a hundred and sixty million, and Markio got that duffle bag with him. You already know what that means."

"I do," Blicky nodded.

"On top of that, the woman whose company made those cameras you complained about a minute ago is up there too."

"Johnna Broward?"

"The one and only. She's dating that actor who plays Tariq on *4Nem* .They're both up there. Juice and Bubbles and the Wilkins twins are up there, Twista's here. YoungNya and her whole lil Plush Gang clique pulled up when Prinny got here. And I ain't even gon' mention who else just got here."

"Who? Whooo?" Blicky Nicky hooted as she took hold of Kitty Jae's shoulders and gave her a vehement shake. A tiny smile danced at the corners of her mouth. "Tell me who. And you bett' not say it's Alexus or Bulletface."

"I won't say it's Alexus or Bulletface." Kitty's smile brightened as Blicky's dimmed. "It's more like Alexus *and* Bulletface."

That did it. Blaire. "Blicky Nicky" Ketchum threw her head back and screamed for all she was worth. She ran in place. She jumped for joy. One of the girls in the locker room yelled that she had just seen Prinny standing out in the hallway with Queen A and Bulletface, and that news inspired a second ululant shriek of joy from Blicky. Kitty Jae actually laughed. She had to grip Blicky's wrist in both hands and anchor herself to keep Blicky from running out of restroom to get a glimpse of the famous A-list couple.

"Girl, calm down."

"Let me gooo."

"Are you going to behave? Can you put that whole situation with Shmoney Rose to the side so we can get to the bag?"

Blicky sucked her teeth and spun back to look at Kitty Jae. Her lips were so full that people often accused her of receiving lip injections. Her costume was barely a costume at all, just a pair of glittery pink stars pasted over her nipples, a pink and white Fendi thong, and pink-sequined six-inch heels.

"I'll leave it alone— for tonight," she said, and wrenched loose of Kitty's firm grip. "But this shit is far from over."

"Deal."

"Come on, ho."

Blicky turned and hurried out to the locker room with Kitty Jae right behind her. It was a big red room with thick red carpeting, a crescent-shaped red leather sectional sofa, and red steel smart lockers lining one wall and half of another. The sofa sat in the sunken area of the room, and it faced a massive 120-inch widescreen TV. The coffee table was a slab of glass laid flat over a realistic sculpture of Cardi B on all fours. Two more TVs hung on the opposite wall.

Most of the girls were grouped around the hallway door, staring out with wide eyes an gaping smiles. Aqua, Thick Doll, and Kimmy Kakes, had arrived; they were at their lockers, rushing to get dressed. Shmoney and Cherish were standing at Shmoney's open locker, both of them acting like they weren't watching Blicky.

Fat Perry had come over to stand beside Adonis. Wide-faced and bald, he had a jumbo body that was almost perfectly round. His ears, nose, and lips were incredibly small compared to the size of his head. He resembled a great brown land turtle in his tight black SECURITY shirt and stretchy black cotton pants.

"Get off that bullshit, Blicky, " he said, extending an arm to block her from passing him. "I'll throw yo' lil ass right out that back door."

Blicky went from staring expectantly at the crowded hallway door to regarding Fat Perry with cold contempt.

"Somebody needs to throw yo' big ass right on a diet," she replied in the calmest of tones. "Stay outta my business, beach ball. Me and Shmoney got a date, but it won't be tonight. Not with Bulletface in the buildin'."

"I got her," Kitty Jae said, suppressing a laugh. "She'll be good. Y'all got my word."

"Better watch that smart as mouth," Perry warned.

"Better watch that calorie intake," Blicky countered. She gave a triumphant smirk and walked around the big man just as Big Gabby's fear-inducing voice boomed from somewhere out in the hallway and sent the crowd of nosey strippers hurrying back into the room.

The boss lady appeared in the doorway a moment later. She was at least fifty pounds heavier than she'd been before her pork-faced superior was blown to bacon bits. She must have had her dress custom made, because it fit her like a latex glove.

What the hell y'all think this is, a circus? Back the hell up. Act like y'all got some sense."

Her authoritative tone got immediate results. The girls who'd already backed away from the doorway moved to put even more space between themselves and Big Gabby. She didn't have to turn sideways to squeeze through the doorway, but her elbows and hips made contact with the door frame on both sides as she wobbled into the room.

A collective gasp swept through the locker room when Big Gabby stepped aside and Princess Kelly walked in with Alexus Costilla and YoungNya right behind her.

"Queen A!" shrieked Dana "Gold Body" Armstrong, a sexy silver-haired redbone transplanted from the south side of Milwaukee, Wisconsin.

The shout set off a momentary round of applause that would have lasted a lot longer had the girls not raised their smartphones. Kitty Jae was one of them. Big Gabby's hard, authoritative eyes scanned the room until they landed on Blicky, at which point she pointed and said, "*You* need to calm down."

"I'm calm, I'm calm." Blicky held up her hands in a show of surrender. "I swear I'm done." She was just as starstruck as the rest of the girls, her eyes unwaveringly glued to Alexus.

It was a triple celebrity sighting. Princess had made it big in the television industry, YoungNya was among the most talented female lyricist to ever come out of Chicago, and Alexus Costilla had the kid of wealth a regular person could not even *dream* of possessing.

"Y'all ready to turn up?" Prinny asked the room. She grinned at the chorus of elongated Yeahs. "Okay, okay. That's the energy I wanna see I hope y'all got some money counters on deck, because tonight y'all gon' need it."

The Mexican man who entered the room with Alexus was so tall that he had to duck to get through the doorway. He wore an impeccable white business suit and Alexus was wrapped in a snow-white fur coat that covered her from throat to toe.

When the girls stopped screaming over Prinny's promising announcement, Alexus said, "I just wired Gabby a million dollars to split between all Prime Shifters. No strings attached. I hope that helps. "

Tears spilled at this second announcement. Joyful statements of gratitude were shouted. There were thirty dancers assigned to Prime Shift, which meant each of them would be receiving a little over thirty-three thousand dollars. And that was on top of whatever they made during their shift.

Alexus parted her pretty lips in a smile that showcased two rows of perfectly square white teeth. Her lustrous black hair was fashioned into five neat cornrows that came together in a thick braid at the base of her skull and slithered around to her right shoulder. Her skin complexion was like burnished copper, and there was a phosphorescent glow to it that made her appear more angelic than human. Her eyes were the verdant color of freshly picked limes, and there was a wintery chill to her seemingly warmhearted stare, as if those limes had spent a few hours in a freezer before settling in between their lashy eyelids.

They landed on Kitty and froze her in place.

"She lookin' atchoo!" Blicky Nicky said in wavering tones of astonishment. "Sis! Sis! Jaresha! She lookin' atchoo!"

"I heard you the first time."

"Didn't act like it."

"I hope Shmoney Rose busts you upside your head."

'Psshh. Girl, please. I told you my daddy was a boxer when he was younger, Taught me all da moves. I'll uppercut that ho like Craig did Deebo. Just *bam!*" She tried to uppercut the palm of her left hand, ended up only grazing it, and accidentally punched herself on the chin.

Kitty Jae choked on a laugh as Blicky frowned and massaged her throbbing chin, She was about to call Blicky a dumbass bitch when Big Gabby bellowed like she had a bullhorn stuck in her throat.

"Okay, y'all. Gather round. Group photo. Jayda, you get over there and take the picture. And take a few of em."

The huge width of Big Gabby's body had completely eclipsed the petite young woman who came around from behind her. Jayda used a fingertip to shove her eyeglasses up the bridge of her nose as she crossed the room to stand behind the sofa.

All the girls wanted to get as close to Queen A and YoungNya as they possibly could, and since Kitty Jae and Blicky Nicky were way over near the restroom door when the frantic positioning began, they ended up far away from where Alexus, Princess, and Nya stood beneath the television. They posed and smiled from the very end of the line of posers., their eyes on Jayda's smartphone, their backs to the open hallway door behind them.

Many of the girls were still jockeying for position when Blicky happened to glace back over her shoulder. Her eyes got big, her brow went up and she gasped.

"Ohmahgod," she said.

"What?" Kitty looked back, saw what Blicky was seeing, and gasped like Blicky had gasped. 'Ohmahgod!"

Standing there in the hallway was Blake "Bulletface" King.

His people, Prinny's people, and Nya's Plush Gang girls had merged into one big entourage. Bulletface was grinning in a way that exposed just a few of his diamond encrusted teeth. His red Givenchy hoodie complimented the thread in his fitted designer jeans and the all-red Air Jordan 5's on his feet. The twin dimples in his cheek were permanent reminders of the two bullets he'd taken to the face more than a decade ago; aside from those age-old gunshot wounds, his rich dark skin was without a blemish.

"You two on the end," Jayda said, "I'ma need y'all to look this way,"

Reluctantly, Kitty Jae looked forward. So did Blicky Nicky. Jayda was a happy photographer. Cherish Taylor and Shmoney Rose, dressed like slutty cowgirls in wide-brimmed cowboy hats, and frilled costumes, squatted low in front of Alexus with their tongues pushed out and their hands on their boobs. Alexus opened her fur to reveal a skintight Balenciaga print catsuit that was as white as her coat. Kitty had forgotten all about the MTN cameramen until one of them moved to get a better view.

She briefly wondered if their footage would make it onto the show.

Then her thoughts tiptoed back to the billionaire rap star who was standing in the hallway behind her. She'd fantasized about fucking him too many times to enumerate, and despite the fact that his gorgeous superstar of a wife was just a few feet to her right, those long forgotten fantasies returned with all the clarity of a three dimensional movie.

It was four minutes till ten when Jayda finished taking pictures. Most of the girls went to their lockers to put away their phones and other things before the start of their shift. Kitty and Blicky had neighboring lockers – which was how they'd become acquainted to begin with – and when Kitty reached up top to slip her phone into her purse. Blicky saw that her watch was missing.

"Where yo' time?" Blicky asked, proving once again that crazy questions formulate in the minds of crazy people.

"Forgot it at home." Kitty Jae didn't feel like going into the whole robbery story three minutes before her shift started. "Bulletface was lookin' good, wasn't he?"

Blicky Nicky was digging around in her Chanel handbag, but they both turned to look out the hallway door. Bulletface was no longer in their line of sight. Alexus and YoungNya had left out, as had Gabby and her bespectacled sidekick, but the hallway was still crowded. Prinny was standing just outside the open doorway, staring up into the eyes of a tall, strongly built man with thick dreadlocks and a handsome smile.

"I honestly don't know how Alexus does it," Blicky said. She emphasized the last four words with perfect enunciation. "I couldn't marry no nigga dat fine. I would fuck him to death, and I mean that in the most literal way, Here." She wrested a diamond Cartier watch away from a clinging hair extension in her purse and offered it to Kitty. "Wear this one. I'll get it back tomorrow."

Kitty Jae would have declined the offer if she hadn't switched focus to Prinny's mystery man. Three or four of the other girls were holding up their phones, recording video of the intimate encounter, video that would likely make the rounds on social media before surfacing on the Shad Room and TMZ.

"Who is he?' Blicky asked, following Kitty's gaze.

"I don't know. I ain't never seen him before. Least I don't think I have. He cute. though."

"Definitely is."

"Markio gon' be pissed." Kitty Jae clasped the borrowed watch around her waist and closed her locker. "He was really in love with Prinny. You know he had moved her into his mansion and everything."

"Yeah, and then he *fucked her sister!* The hell kinda love is that? I wish a nigga would be in a whole relationship with me and then go and fuck one of my sisters."

"What would you do?" Kitty asked with an eagerly expectant smirk. Because coming up with things to do to people she hated was something Blicky Nicky excelled at.

"I'd cut off his dick, throw it in a blender, turn it up on high...maybe add in some berries. And there you go. Have me a Blackberry Big Dick Smoothie." Her pretty Puerto Rican Face lit up at the idea. "Bet he wouldn't fuck *another* one of my sisters."

Kitty Jae snickered her amusement.

"It's about that time, y'all" Cherish Taylor said. "Let's get it. Huddle up."

She motioned for all the girls – collectively known as the Prime Time Girls – to join her beside the Cardi B table. Every night before the start of their shift they all got together for a ritualistic chant that one of their long gone predecessors had ripped off from Sunset Park, a decades old movie Kitty Jae had never even seen. *The Prime Time* Girls had put their own motivational spin on the mantra, and Cherish Taylor, the self-appointed president of PTG, was always the one who got it started.

Cherish shouted. *"Prime Time Girls, what time is it?"*

The others screamed. *"It's time to shake ass! It's time to pay the rent!"* And when Cherish repeated the question, the rest of the girls delivered their second and final line. *"It's time to do some tricks! Bounce on a nigga dick!"* After that they all yelled "Ayyyy!" and made their asses bounce and wiggle.

The result was galvanizing. Kitty Jae's heart started pumping blood at a fast pace. She was like an electric vehicle fresh off the charging station, all juiced up and ready to roll.

Leaving the locker room, exactly half of the girls broke away from the line to pass through the health and fitness spa and out through the less exclusive Preferred Shift locker room to the main floor. Kitty Kakes and Thick Doll were among them, as they were scheduled to perform on the main stage while YoungNya flaunted her lyrical prowess on the mic. The remaining fifteen continued on through the stairwell door and up to the VIP Lounge.

It was time to shake ass.

Chapter 11

Some people were book smart yet ignorant enough to stomp, jump and flip through the minefield of the streets.

Princess Kelly was not one of them.

Knowing that Millionaire Markio and FBS were fifteen-deep in the VIP Lounge, and also that Bulletface, a longtime member of the TVL brotherhood, would likely side with Markio if trouble arose between him and the Stones, Prinny had led L-Stone and the rest of the men in his gang down the blue-carpeted hallway of private rooms – now called VIP Suites – and into the much larger room at the far end of the hall that had once been Weezy's office but was now called the Luxury Suites.

The walls were the same cobalt blue as the wall-to-wall carpet and the overstuffed, semicircular sofa was the darker blue that white people turned when they were dead too long. A sparkly golden pole was bolted to the ceiling and the center of the floor. The varying costs of using the Luxury Suite were posted on the wall outside the door, but Prinny needn't have read it, because one of the Wilkins twins came speed-walking up the hallway on high Louboutin heels and caught up with Prinny before L-Stone and his boys could even make it to the sofa.

L-Stone sat down in the middle of the sofa, doing something on his iPhone. Braylon, Monk, and Keymo, having already crossed the Luxury Suite threshold, turned and stared at the beautiful young woman who'd rushed up behind them.

"Y'all might wanna use a different room," the Wilkins twin said. She had lovely hazel eyes. "This is our most expensive suit. Costs between three and five thousand dollars per hour, depending on the package you choose. Oh, and that's per person."

Furrowing her brow, Prinny took a moment to read over the wall-mounted advertising placard:

$3,000 Luxury Suite Gold Package: 1 Hour Private Dance in Luxury Suite, Bottle of Dom Perignon or Premium "Half" Bottle, Free Transportation to Hotel

$5,000 Luxury Suite Platinum Package: 1 Hour Private Dance, Bottle of Dom Perignon 2009 or Louis Roederer (Cristal), Free Transportation to Hotel

"Wow," Prinny said, digging down in her purse. 'Wish they had this when I danced here. How much of the money goes to the entertainer?"

"The House only takes a thousand." Hazel Eyes looked in at the four Black P Stones, then back at Zoodie, who was standing behind Prinny. "Per person, I mean. One dancer for each guest."

Prinny nodded her head and took the two remaining stacks of hundreds out of her purse. "Platinum Package for all four of my bros in there. And make sure you send in some real baddies." She handed over the cash and then leaned into the Luxury Suite to pull the door shut before adding, "Make sure they stay in there. Do not, under any circumstances, allow them to go back out into the stairwell without me being present, and if either one of Markio's boys comes down this hallway for a private dance, do your best to keep my boys from seeing them."

The VIP host squinted. A glimmer of trepidation flickered across her sweet hazel eyes. Her grip on the pile of cash loosened, as if she feared that all those brand-new hundred-dollar bills were coated in anthrax or some other transmissible disease.

Down at the opposite end of the corridor, Nishelle and Asia were laughing with one of the bouncers who'd steeped out of the glassed-in security booth across from the elevators. The muffled shouts of the Prime Time Girls could be heard beyond the closed stairwell door as they climbed the stairs.

"Why can't they see each other?" Hazel Eyes asked. Her long tight skirt looked like it was made of goldfish scales, and her silk voile bandage top was white and transparent enough to see right through to her lacey white bra. "They don't like each other or some'n?"

"You could say that" Prinny said, and that was all she was willing to say.

She turned and headed back down the hallway, checking her phone to see if Markio had read her reply to his last message—Nobody you'd know, she'd texted— and to see if he'd written her back.

He'd read it, but he had yet to reply.

"Damn, you look so good in that outfit," Zoodie said.

The compliment was a confidence boost Prinny didn't even know she needed, sweet words that filled her spirit with warm delight.

Zoodie was keeping step alongside her, making sure to stay a foot or two behind to get an eyeful of her sauntering derriere. She looked back at him with an appreciative smirk that spread into an even more appreciative smile when she saw that he was biting down on the center of his bottom lip and staring hungrily at her lower half.

"Thank you," she said, in the high-pitched intonation of a lovestruck teen.

"No. No. Thank you. Thank you for thinking of me on this very special day. I'll never forget it."

Prinny slowed her steps before coming to a complete stop and spinning to face her mocha-skinned date. He immediately took advantage of the stop, placing his big hands on her hips and dipping in for a fleeting smooch.

"What's on your mind?" Zoodie asked, like Facebook's prompt for a status update.

"You," Prinny said. Which wasn't necessarily a lie. She'd been thinking of launching her phone at Markio's forehead for not replying to her text, but Zoodie's well-timed compliment had shifted her thoughts back to him.

Unsurprisingly, his hands moved from her hips to her ass. He sucked in a breath as he squeezed.

"You gon' fuck around and make me fall in love," he said.

"Is that a bad thing?"

"I don't know. Time'll tell, I guess." He glanced toward the Luxury Suite. "What's the deal with them and Markio?"

"It's a long story. To make it short, the man who was the General before L-Stone owed Markio a lot of money and decided he wasn't going to pay the debt. His name was Jesse Harris, but they called him Baby Stone. He was my baby daddy's best friend."

"What happened to him? Was he killed?"

Prinny gave a barely discernible nod. "Right in front of his fiancée too. Shooters jumped out of two white SUVs. One guy stood over him and shot him a bunch of times in the head. Happened on Fifty-third and Prairie, a few blocks away from the apartment building I lived in until I was thirteen. Three other boys got killed with him."

"And you all think Markio did it."

"No. He was at my place, That's the day I met Alexus, the day I signed on to produce The Real Baddies."

"But you believe he had somebody else do it."

"I know he did," Prinny said, with real conviction. "I even know who did it. I didn't know at first, he never fessed up to it or anything, but Alexus told me the truth. It was him. He paid a million dollars for the hit. Which, you know, is pocket change to him."

Asia sucked her teeth from twenty feet away, and Nishelle said, "Girl, will y'all come on? I ain't get all dressed up to stand in the hallway."

Prinny and Zoodie were all smiles as they continued on down the hallway, her right hand interlaced with his left hand. She was so happy that, if not for the heels she might have skipped her way to her waiting friends.

"I gotta have a talk with Markio when we get in the VIP Lounge," she said to Zoodie. "Not about anything... you know..."

"I know. About that whole Tramell situation."

"Yeah."

"I figured as much." He let his shoulder jump. "Do your thing. I'm not really the jealous type – for the most part, at least. In my experience, it's usually me who gets berated for being too friendly with an ex."

"Hm" Prinny cut a glance at her trusting companion. Her eyelids narrowed shakily, as if she were facing a stiff wind.

Zoodie put on a fool's grin and gave Prinny a light pat on the ass. His blackberry visage was enhanced by lips that had never lost a thing from his African ancestors.

A vision arose in Prinny's mind that saw her kissing those amazing full lips while the two of them stood before a pine wood altar, him in a black silk tuxedo, her in a flowery white wedding gown with a detachable train she could tear off for their first dance.

The sudden chime of an arriving elevator snapped Prinny out of the heartwarming reverie. She and Zoodie were half a yard away from Shell and Asia, who were already pushing open the stairwell door to cross the hall and enter the VIP Lounge, when the chrome elevator doors to Prinny's left slid open.

Three hale strippers exited the elevator with three older men in tow. The dancers reacted excitedly to seeing Princess; their eyes got really big, and one of them even gasped.

"Shit, girl, that's Princess," said one dancer.

"Can't wait for season three!" said another.

Prinny smiled and waved an went out through the stairwell door. She said hey to Tank, the thick-bearded bouncer who guarded the VIP Lounge door. Asia told him he looked like Mark Henry, which must have been a compliment, because it raised the edges of the big guy's mouth.

"This your new man?" Tank asked Prinny in his gruff baritone. He and Zoodie were roughly the same height, and they were too busy staring each other down for Tank to see Prinny's briskly nodded reply.

"Yes," Prinny said, to get the jealous bouncers' eyes back on hers. "Zoodie, this is Tank. Tank, this is my boyfriend Zoodie. Tank used to look after me when I danced here. A couple of the girls got robbed in the parking lot, so he would walk me and Aqua out to our cars and trail us for a couple of blocks to make sure we weren't being followed."

"That's right. Princess was always my favorite." He said that to Zoodie as he removed the lanyard from around his beefy neck and used its attached keycard to open the door to the VIP Lounge. Then he looked down at Prinny, showed her all his tobacco-stained front teeth, and said, "I'm proud'a you. Keep it up."

Asia sucked her side teeth and pushed through the door, too eager to get the turn up started to listen to any more of Mark Henry's BS.

Chapter 12

Blicky Nicky was holding her knees and making her butt cheeks bounce like crazy in front of Millionaire Markio and his Fin Ball Shortiez gang, who were all seated along the sofa behind her, when she looked forward and saw Princess enter the VIP Lounge from the stairwell door with her two best friends leading the way and her new boo following in behind her.

The girls who'd managed to finagle their way into Millionaire Markio's section were all gorgeous and shapely, and Markio had the prettiest one in the bunch wedged between him and his boy Gucci Ball. She was mulatto yellow with long curly hair and sharp bejeweled fingernails, wearing a lime green dress that ended four inches above the knee. She kept letting Markio pour Casamigos in her mouth. Every couple of seconds she'd take a pile of dollars off his table and swipe them off the palm of her hand aiming for Blicky and Kitty Jae who was making her fat jiggly ass clap to the beat of YoungNya's "When We Pop Out" as the hot young femcee performed it on the stage below.

Like the great majority of Black America, Blicky Nicky was well aware of the cheating scandal that had brought Prinny and Markio's year-long relationship to an acrimonious end.

A fiend for drama – for action of any kind, really – Blicky took great joy in looking back at Markio to gauge his reaction to Prinny's arrival.

She was not disappointed.

Gucci Ball reached around the pretty girl's back and tapped Markio on the shoulder. "Lord! There go ya girl," he said, shouting over the music.

Markio would have been hard pressed not to look, because every pair of eyes in the VIP Lounge looked. There were four cameramen filming the cast of *The Real Baddies of Chicago* as they danced for dollars; three of those cameras panned over to watch Prinny as she made her way to her reserved section.

Three or four conflicting emotions flashed across Markio's remarkably handsome features, the first of which was the pure and unrestrained joy of seeing Prinny stalk proudly across the room after having gone so many months without seeing her at all. His whole face smiled; it wasn't just his mouth and cheeks but also his eyes and the way his brow moved up on his forehead. Then his lifted brow wrinkled with despair when he realized that the man walking behind Prinny was holding her hand. His face hardened into a mask of contempt after that, the outermost parts of it seeming to merge toward his medium sized nose. Finally his smile returned, but there was nothing behind it. That smile was a five-star hotel suite with nobody in it— just vacant.

Blicky Nicky giggled at his misery.

The sofas in the VIP Lounge were longer than the tables, though not by much. Just about every seated patron had at least one diamond necklace and an iced out watch to go with it. Memphis rap legend Yo Gotti sat behind one table with a few of his CMG artists and some other men Blicky had never seen. Fly Guy Mitchell had brought along two of his Bulls teammates. YoungNya's all-female Plush Gang crew were seated with Johnna Broward, the billionaire tech mogul who was legally Nya's sister-in-law. Half a dozen male and female porn actors occupied the table Kitty Jae had reserved for her two sisters and their cousin Tammy, neither of whom had showed, Big Gabby's fiancé, Tyrone Steele, was among the porn stars, and it came as no surprise that Bunny XXX, a porn star herself, was bouncing her apple bottom in their section.

Every section had at least five to ten thousand dollars in ones to throw. Most had a lot more. Blicky and Kitty Jae had chosen wisely, as Millionaire Markio and FBS had ordered up a combined $90,000 in one-dollar bills, about eight or nine thousand of which was already sprinkled around Blicky Nicky and Kitty Jae's stripper heels.

Blicky flicked her eyes toward the stairwell door as it swung outward again. Big Gabby swayed in first, followed by the tall, stern-faced Mexican man who was always somewhere in Alexus Costilla's shadow. He lowered his unfortunately shaped head to keep the pate of his skull from making contact with the top of the door frame. Once in, he looked both ways presumably surveying the room for threats and then both he and Big Gabby turned toward the open doorway.

They watched Alexus Costilla step into the room as if they feared she might stumble over the threshold and fall to her knee. Three of Queen A's besties came in behind her; high powered attorney Nikkia Staples, retired attorney Britney Bostic, and celebrity marriage counselor Dr. Melanie Farr. Then came Queen A's daughter Vari; Gabby's new personal assistant, Jayda; and four more Mexican men in white business suits.

DJ Ickyz took that moment to announce Queen A's arrival over the loudspeaker. All around the VIP lounge people started picking up their phones and streaming video of Alexus and her girls as she strode unsmilingly toward her two reserved tables, pausing along the way to hug and greet Johnna and the beautiful ladies of Plush Gang, and again to speak briefly with Princess, who then left her own table to join the Costilla train.

Blicky looked away as Prinny was sitting down next to the world's richest woman, not only because Shmoney Rose and Cherish Taylor were walking toward that section but because she wanted to see if Bulletface was coming in through the stairwell door next. He didn't, but there were two more white-suited Mexican men, one with a gnarly scar on the left side of his face, standing there in the open doorway. After a few seconds of watching the room, they moved back and shut the door, but not before Blicky Nicky was able to glimpse three more brown men in white standing on the steps behind them.

When the burgeoning inclination to talk became too heavy a burden for Blicky to bear, she looked at Kitty Jae and said, "I wonder where Bulletface at."

"Prob'ly getting' ready to perform," Kitty said.

They both swiveled their heads to peer through the glass and down at the stage on the main floor below. YoungNya was still spitting her nefarious gangster rhymes into a mic. The song, 'West Side Nights,' featured FendiDa Rappa, who'd joined Nya onstage as a surprise guest performer.

The ugly young man called Gucci Ball reached up and closed his sweaty hand around Blicky's pinkie finger. His charcoal lips peeled back to reveal twin rows of diamond encrusted teeth. Blicky had once read that there were no such thing as truly black eyes, but Gucci Ball was the exception. His irises blended with his pupils. Either that or he had the most dilated pupils in the history of mankind.

"You ain't answered none'a my texts," he said.

'Why dey call you Gucci Ball?" Blicky asked. "What, they tryna say you look like Gucci Mane or some'n? 'Cause you don't. You really don't. You look more like a French bulldog wit' diamond teef"

Millionaire Markio and the fat man seated to his right fell against each other and laughed The girl in the lime green dress laughed too.

"That why you ain't replied to my texts? I ain't attractive enough for you? Or is it 'cause you on TV now, done got too famous to fuck on a street nigga?"

"Attractive *enough*? Attractive *enough*? " Blicky's head rocked side to side every time she said it. "Boy, you ain't attractive *at all*. Not even a little bit. But that ain't got shit to do with it. I done fucked some ugly niggas before. A dick ain't got no face."

"Then what's the issue? Or did you just put your number in my phone so you could steal that video you sent to TMZ?"

The close-mouthed smirk Blicky gave Gucci Ball betrayed her guilt. She'd been at the House of Lords, Millionaire Markio's Lincoln Park mega mansion, on the night Prinny had arrived to find her sister planted on Markio's lap. Gucci Ball had recorded video of Prinny planted on Markio's lap. Gucci Ball had recorded video of Prinny confronting Markio in his twenty-car garage, cursing him with the foulest possible language, and just as Gucci Ball alleged, Blicky had sneakily messaged herself the video when she was supposed to be only saving her number to his list of contacts. She'd sent the video to both TMZ and The Shade Room. It went viral within minutes.

"Yeeaah," Gucci Ball said, bobbing his ugly head. "Thought I ain't know about that, huh?"

Blicky Nicky rolled her eyes and was about to get back to dancing when Gucci Ball offered her a deal that took her completely by surprise, mainly because she had no idea what he was talking about.

"Aight. Aight. Check this out," he said dragging a healthy wad of cash out from the left hand pocket of his designer jeans. "I'll give you two bands, *and* I'll find out who robbed your girl Kitty Jae for her watch and get it back. All you gotta do is…"

Gucci Ball finished making his offer, but the end of it didn't register in Blicky's brain because she was raising her head to stare at Kitty Jae through tightly squinted eyelids.

"Jaresha," she said. "The hell is he talkin' about?"

"Huh?" Kitty looked guilty as OJ Simpson.

"Bitch, you heard me. What the hell is he talkin' about? I thought you told me you left that watch at home. You got robbed?" She offered no time for a reply. "I hate liars. Don't fuckin' lie to me, Jaresha. I saved your boyfriend's *life* a few months ago. Saved his motheruckin' *life*! And yet you wanna lie to me."

"We'll talk about it later, after we count up this money."

"No." Blicky had already stopped shaking her ass. She was glaring at Kitty Jae with her head turned slightly to the side in an untrusting gesture of skepticism. "No, no, no, no. We gon' talk about this now. We gon' talk about his shit right … the fuck.. now."

Kitty Jae shook her head no. The shake was more of a twitch, barely discernible to the human eye unless you knew what you were looking for. That spasmodic headshake spawned an unbridle rage within Blicky Nicky that was about as grotesque as Gucci Ball's heavily pockmarked face.

And Shmoney Rose chose that precise moment to step in between Blicky Nicky and Kitty Jae.

It was the purest example of a person being at the wrong place, at the wrong time.

"Excuse me, Markio," Shmoney said. "Alexus and Princess would like to have a word with you when you get a sec—.

A Casamigos bottle Blicky Nicky snatched up from Markio's table came down on the back of Shmoney Rose head before she could voice the last syllable in the word *second*.

Tink! The bottle sang off Shmoney's pretty skull, as if calling out for a soulful duet with the R&B songstress of the same name.

Shmoney Rose stumbled sideways and fell forward against Gucci Ball. Blicky went after her, raising the bottle for another swing, but this time when she brought the bottle down it slipped from her grasp and struck the ear of a cute girl who was seated across the lap of one of the FBS members a few seats down.

The cute girl wore a red wrap dress that was as tight and short as the lime green one her friend wore. She grabbed her ear and grimaced at the sudden pain she felt there. Her pretty brown eyes looked down at the unbroken bottle and then up at the woman who'd thrown it. Two seconds later she hopped off her guy's knee and ran at Blicky Nicky, just as Blicky Nicky was reaching out to get a hand of Shmoney's expensive blond wig.

Blicky had just enough time to get a grip on the blood-slickened hair on one side of Shmoney's head and deliver two hard blows to the other side. Shmoney Rose's pained yelps brought a triumphant sneer to Blicky Nikcy's lips.

She was hauling her fist back for another swing when the girl in the red dress got on her.

"You wanna throw bottles?"

The shouted question came with a side order of rapidly thrown punches, all of which landed just outside of Blicky's right eye. She shut the attacked eye in a defensive wince and ducked away from the girl in the red dress, only to find herself under attact from the girl in the lime green dress on her left side.

"Okay. Okay, bitch," Blicky said, her winning sneer expanding into a hellish malevolent smile. "We can get it on like Donkey Kong!"

She came up at the girl in the lime green dress with a well-aimed uppercut that caught the girl under the chin and lifted her nearly off the cash littered floor. The girl's arms went out to her sides, like an eagle speaking her wings in preparation of flight, and Blicky spun around to confront her initial attacker.

But there was no need for concern.

The girl in the red dress was already sitting on the floor, leaning back on her right hand, holding her left hand over her left eye and staring up at Kitty Jae with her right eye. Her hair stuck up in a way that showed it had been violently pulled. The icy look in her staring eyes said she wanted to get up and fight but was too afraid of getting knocked back down to try it.

Blicky Nicky was turning her attention back to Shmoney Rose when she was suddenly picked up from behind and she knew from the strength of his arms and the scent of his cologne that it was Adonis who'd snatched her up.

"I told y'all!" Blicky Nicky said, pointing at no one in particular as three more bouncers rushed into Millionaire Markio's section – one to drag Kitty Jae away from the seven or eight other girls who were coming to the defense of their two beaten friends, while the second and third bouncers came to Shmoney's aid and warned the two pretty girls to stay back. "I told y'all I was gon' catch that ho! Blabbermouth *that*, you sneak-dissin' ass bitch! Fuck you thought this was?"

And then, as Adonis was carrying her off toward the stairwell door, cradling her sideways against his muscle-stuffed chest as he tried and failed to wriggle out of his powerful arms. Blicky Nicky smiled at all the stunned, staring VIP Lounge patrons and started rapping the words she'd freestyled earlier:

"Friday night at *ten*… Hit that ho in the *chin*…. She won't speak *again*… Hey, hey, hey HEY!"

Chapter 13

Alexus Costilla was smiling.

As one of the most famous faces on the planet, she'd long ago learned the art of masking her emotions. You'd have to know her to read her expressions when she was making a real effort to conceal them. Prinny had gotten to know her. She saw how the billionaire's eyes had grown larger upon witnessing Blicky Nkcy's sudden attack on Shmoney Rose, and how her cheeks grew fuller when Blicky's uppercut knocked the girl in the lime green dress out cold, and how her beautifully groomed eyebrows went up when Kitty Jae hooked the other girl in the eye and threw her to the floor.

"Maybe we should've just waved for him to come over," Alexus said, She made a noise in her throat that sounded like a hiccup. "That went terribly wrong."

"I told you that girl was crazy," Prinny said.

"Oh, she's ten miles past crazy. Did you see that punch? "She just KO"d that girl with an uppercut."

The girl in the lime green dress was just waking up. Her friends were helping her up, while the bouncers ordered all the girls in Markio's section to take the stairs at the front of the VIP Lounge down to the main floor.

Cherish Taylor had rushed over to help get Shmoney out through the rear stairwell door and downstairs to the health and fitness spa for treatment. There were two full-time registered nurses down there to tend to the girls' medical needs, and Shmoney would be needing both of them. All of her blond hair had gone red with blood by the time she staggered out into the stairwell with Fat Perry holding her close for support. Big Gabby had followed them out.

"I didn't expect that at all," Alexus said, fingering the end of her long black braid.

"Yeah you did." Prinny regarded Alexus with an accusatory side-eye. "That's why you asked Shmoney to go over there in the first place. You wanted to see some drama."

"She hit that ho with a nasty uppercut." Alexus flashed her ivory white teeth. "We're putting that in the season finale. We have to. It's what all the folks in Hollywood call TV gold."

That was Alexus Costilla to a letter. Everything was about ratings with her. High ratings brought in more sponsors, and more sponsors meant more money.

Two new Prime Time Girls came over to replace Shmoney and Cherish. Their stage names were Byooty and Plinni Munni. The table had already been piled high with cash before Alexus walked through the door – $200,000 in one-dollar bills, all bundled in packets of a hundred – and the billionaire's teenage daughter, Savaria King, wasn't wasting any time in getting rid of it, Every few seconds she'd whip a big handful of dollars into the air.

Kitty Jae was back in Markio's section the moment his groupies were gone. Seconds later Aqua went over and joined her.

Which was when Millionaire Markio finally got up and started making his way toward Alexus and Prinny.

"Uh-oh. Here he comes," Alexus said. Her secret smile returned.

The first thing that rose to Prinny's lips was *fuck him and the horse he rode in on*. What she said was, "I hope to God, he can help me without getting me involved. Shit. I don't wanna go to prison."

Alexus furrowed her brow and gave Prinny a look. After checking to see that there was no small microphone clipped to Prinny's sexy Balenciaga bodysuit, she said, "You still haven't told me what that problem is. You know I'm great at problem solving."

Markio approached with his arms outstretched and Alexus stood to embrace him. Prinny was the next to stand. She smiled with just her lips and pretended she was happy to see the ex who'd fucked her sister. Even so, she could not deny the red hot lust that washed through her like a river of fire when he put an arm around her waist and pulled her close for a friendly hug. Their sexual chemistry had always been off the charts, and so her body reacted the way it always had.

She hated him in her heart, but her pussy was still madly in love with him.

There was an elevated platform between each sofa on their side of the room, so that the VIP guest could watch the stage below. The platform was wide enough to fit ten or twelve people comfortably.

"Let's step over here," Alexus said, titling her head toward the platform, "Blake's about to perform in a few minutes."Once on the platform with their backs to the two remaining cameraman – the other two had rushed out behind Blicky Nicky and Shmoney – Alexus, Markio, and Princess squandered a couple of second watching the rap performance. FendiDa Rappa was now rapping her own song, "Point Me 2," and it seemed like the whole club was rapping it with her:

He off a pill, nigga ill, is it even real?
He got a glizzy wit' no bullets, do he even kill?....

Princess was halfway tempted to rap along with everyone else. Instead she leaned in toward Alexus and Markio, cupped her hand over her mouth, and said. "My girl Sadé, her boyfriend keeps trying to get her to turn me in for a murder." Then almost as an afterthought, she added, "A murder I had absolutely nothing to do with."

"Sadé?" Markio had his Styrofoam cup in front of his mouth as he spoke, "Sadé who?"

"Dobbs. Sadé Dobbs. She stays over on Fifty-fourth and Hoyne, Her boyfriend's name Tramell. I just left from over there. They were on their way to a backyard R and B party two houses down from theirs."

Markio sipped his drink and nodded his head. He became thoughtful, gazing out over the crowd below with a distant look in his eye. Most of the people down there were focused on the main stage, but a few dozen had turned to look up at the three black celebrities who were standing just behind the VIP Lounge's front glass wall. Some of them were raising their smartphones, to record video and take pictures.

"Operation Dead Eye," Markio said, after a time. "Yeah. Operation Dead Eye. That's what the feds called it when they indicted the GD's off Fifty fourth and Hoyne, I was in the joint when that went down, but I had a subscription to the *Chicago Sun-Times.* I read all about it." He paused to sip some more of his drink. "So Tramell, huh? Fuck is he, a cop or some'n?"

"I don't know what he is. All I know is what Sadé told me, He wanted her to turn me in for the reward money. They've been gettin' high on that gas station weed, and every time they smoke it they get all paranoid. The shit got'em thinkin' their phones are tapped."

"What this nigga look like? And what's the address?"

"I'll text you the address."

"Nahh. Hell nahh." Markio was shaking his head. "Fuck that. Don't text me nothin' about this. Just tell me the address. I'll remember it."

Prinny didn't know the actual address, so she gave him the general description of Sadé's toy strewn backyard, her garage with the big six-pointed star spraypainted on the side, and the color of the house. She used The Street View option on Google Maps to show Markio the front side of the house. After that she brought up Sadé's Facebook page and showed Markio a photo of Tramell.

Thin and lanky, with a receding hairline and a florid brown face, Tramell was a tired- looking man with vapid brown eyes and a nose that nearly spanned the entire length of his narrow head. He was maybe six-two, but he walked with a perpetual stoop that made him appear shorter than he actually was. In the photo he was standing on the fifth rung of an aluminum ladder that was leaned up against the back of Sadé's ramshackle home. He wore a sunshine yellow hard hat tipped back on his skinny head, a threadbare wifebeater with stains and dirt smudges all over it, a tan leather toolbelt that drooped around his bony hips and made his blue Levi's jeans sag down on one side, and brown Timberland boots. He was turned sideways with just the toe of one boot supporting him on the ladder, looking back and regarding the area with a lazy smirk.

Alexus studied the photograph for a long moment. So did Markio. Finaly Alexus gave a small nod, repositioned her braid, and offered her first words on the matter.

"Okay. We got it. It'll be taken care of."

"When, though?" Prinny asked. "What if this nigga dials nine-one-one tonight, right after they leave that party?""Have you tried paying him off?" Alexus smiled and waved at someone down below. Her lips barely moved as she spoke. "How much is that reward he's after?"

"Twelve thousand."

"That's it?" Markio said in disbelief.

"I gave Sadé ten grand before I left and she broke down crying. Said she was done smokin' that shit." Prinny sighed. "I don't know. I don't know what to do. I just know I can't go to jail."

"You won't," Alexus assured her. "Few years ago, there was this team of FBI agents who'd decided Markio and his boys on Sixteenth Street should be their next big bust. They sent in an undercover agent to befriend Markio at one of his book singing events. Tried to get close to him that way. Next thing you know that FBI agent's relatives started getting picked off one by one. Then the senior agent in charge of that gang task force went out for dinner with a known prostitute and woke up to find the whore lying dead in his bed with a knife buried in her chest. Similar situations befell the other task force agents. See where I'm going with this?"

Princess bobbed her head. She saw, all right.

"Markio," Alexus said, "I want you to go and have a chat with Tramell."

"What's the ticket?"

"Half of what you owe."

Whatever that meant wrestled a smile out of Markio. His eyes were downcast. Prinny followed his line of sight to three uniformed police officers on the main floor below. They were walking toward a door that opened into the health and fitness spa. Cherish Taylor was standing there in the open doorway, holding her phone in front of her mouth and beckoning the officers over.

"This bitch done called the po-leece," Markio commented.

Princess hated his smile, hated it because she loved it, so she shifted towards Alexus just as the stunningly beautiful billionaire was putting her own perfect smile on display.

Bulletface had just walked out from behind the towering blue velvet curtains at the rear of the main stage. His appearance was met with a deafening wave of cheers, and he launched right into his opening verse of YoungNya's gold certified single, "Remember Me Now."

Prinny moved closer to Alexus. "I got just one more question," she said.

"Yeah?" Alexus was going to the camera app on her iPhone, to record her husband's performance. "What's that?"

"The old man. Herb. Is he gone for good? I mean, where is he?"

Alexus leaned toward Prinny and whispered the cryptic answer directly in her ear.

Chapter 14

"Ay, Blicky, you might wanna get outta here. Perry say three cops just come in through da front. Two dudes and a chick."

Jigg had leaned into the Prime Shift locker room on his good leg. His serious face was as black as his shirt.

"Fuck twelve. Them bitches can flip upside down and kiss my whole asshole," Blicky said, but that was only because she was already dressed in her favorite jeans and pushing her head through the neckhole in her gray and blue Only the Family hoodie.

She slammed her locker shut and made a beeline for the rarely used exit door that stood beside the last locker in the middle of the back wall. She glanced back only once, because the two widescreen televisions were playing Bulletface and YoungNya's live performance, and Blicky Nicky *loved* Bulletface. Not more than she loved King Von and Chief Keef, but Bulletface was definitely in her top five.

"Good evenin' officers," Jigg said from across the room.

Blicky Nicky's fast-paced walk became an outright run , for she knew that her favorite bouncer's friendly greeting to the police was really a thinly-veiled warning to his favorite dancer.

She slammed through the red-painted steel door with the corners of her thick lips drawn up in an excited smile. Outside, the soles of her blue and white Balenciaga sneakers smacked the wet concrete walkway that ran alongside the building. Fear never entered her brain as she dashed toward the parking lot, not even when she heard the hard footfalls of the pigs pounding the pavement behind her. If anything, she got even more exited.

"Chicago police! Stop running! I'll tase you! Don't fucking make me tase you!"

"Gotta catch me first!"

Blicky giggled merrily and ran on

Her Cybertruck was just a few yards ahead of her, She'd used her smartphone to get the engine going a minute earlier. The Tesla app was still open on her phone screen, and she didn't miss a beat in her run as she raised her phone to unlock her doors.

"You're only makin' it worse! Stop running!"

"Eat my ass, bitch!"

Blicky made it to her driver door, threw it open, climbed in and pulled the door shut three seconds before the officer leading the chase – a tall, bespectacled white man with a bunch of tattoos decorating his muscular forearms – came to a boot sliding stop outside her window. By then she had already locked the doors.

The officer that darted around to the passenger's side door was so black that he and Jigg might have sprouted from the same family tree. He was black like native Africans are black. His head was shaved around the sides and had a mess of spaghetti like dreads spilling down from the top. He had bronze stripes on the collar of his shirt, and he spoke with a heavy accent.

"Open da dooah! Open da dooah!" He knocked at the window with his hard black knuckle. "Titus, get the plate numba!"

The white cop did as he was told.

"Ma'am. Ma'am." The African cop knocked again. "Open da dooah or I break da window."

Blicky giggled and looked straight ahead, There was a third police officer jogging toward her truck, a woman who was short and thick and dark-skinned, though not nearly as black as her sergeant. Blicky knew her name. She was Officer Pierre, a Haitian whose family had migrated to Chicago when she was just a teen. Following a rash of parking lot robberies and one shooting outside of Queen of Diamonds, Mayor Johnson had ordered the Chicago Police Department's third District to assign a group of officers from their community safety team to patrol the area. As a CST member, officer Pierre had made it her mission to become acquainted with all QOD dancers, bouncers, and bartenders.

Desmond Crawford, a Minority Television Network cameraman who'd been following Blicky around ever since she officially joined the cast of The Real Baddies of Chicago, was just a couple of steps behind Officer Pierre, running with his bulky high-tech camera mounted on his shoulder, with two other crewmembers hustling along behind him

Three separate groups of people who were walking to their cars stopped to see what was going on.

Two white Escalades that seemed to have been aimlessly traversing the parking lot slowed to a crawl.

When Titus reappeared at Blicky's window he was holding his nightstick. "Last warning," he said, in the voice that had threatened to tase her a few moments ago. "Step out of the vehicle."

"You sound like Robocop," Blicky said, catching her breath.

Titus swung his mighty nightstick. It struck Blicky's window and bounced right off, not even leaving a mark. Two more strikes got the same result. The Cybertruck's widow proved indestructible.

"Bitch, I'm Ford tough," Blicky said. She laughed at the cop with her nose pressed flat against her window

Turning around in her seat, she reversed out of the parking lot and spun her steering wheel to the right, aiming the rear end of her truck at the front end of Shmoney Rose's hot pink Bentayga. She rammed the Bentley SUV so hard that it went askew and dented the driver door off the darker pink Rolls-Royce Wraith it was parked next to.

Blicky's smile broadened, because that Wraith belonged to Cherish Taylor.

Officer Titus was yelling something into his police radio as Blicky Nicky straightened her wheel and went racing out of the parking lot.

The people who'd stopped to stare were cheering and clapping their hands, while the alarms on the Bentayga and the Wraith screamed out into the night.

Chapter 15

Kitty Jae's eyes got big, her eyelashes fluttered and her lips fell apart when, just thirty-five minutes after Millionaire Markio and his FBS squad suddenly vacated the VIP lounge, L-Stone and his boys walked in.

The four men crossed the floor to Prinny's section and sat down. One of them kissed Prinny's friend, Nishelle, on the lips. The baldheaded one cracked open one of the five fifths of Hennessy that stood on the table amongst a litter of smartphones, designer handbags, and several stacks of one-dollar bills.

"How much you think you done made tonight?"

That was BunnyXXX

Kitty Jae was sitting on a barstool at the bar on the west end of the VIP Lounge, taking her fifteen minute break from dancing. QOD limited its dancers to just two drinks per shift, and Kitty was on her second glass of Patron. She'd been so fixated on L-Stone that she hadn't seen Bunny come over and sit beside her.

Thinking of the money put a grin on Kitty's face. "You know Markio and all the FBS niggas from my neighborhood. They left me with that whole ninety thousand, told me to split it with Blicky's crazy ass. I had to get Adonis and Bee Kay to help me carry all that money down to the locker room."

'I know it was a lot of blood on that money."

"It definitely is."

"Did they tell you she crashed her truck into Shmoney's and then sped off from twelve."

Kitty Jae nodded her head and drank from her straw She'd heard all about Blicky's parking lot antics from Robyn Jarrett, the MTN field producer she'd met at Blicky's west side home a few weeks back. They'd crossed paths in the stairwell about twenty minutes ago, as Kitty was returning from the locker room.

"Yeah, Robyn gave me the whole rundown. She had just spoken with Officer Pierre, They found Blicky's truck abandoned at Auto Zone on Eighty-first and Cottage. Somebody must've gave her a ride."

"Where do you think she went?'

"Hell if I know," Kitty said with a shrug. "Hopefully a mental hospital."

Bunny laughed, and Kitty Jae flexed the fingers of her left hand. Her first two knuckles were a little swollen. She kept switching her gaze from the men in Prinny's section to Bulletface and Alexus.

The A-list celebrity couple sat hip to hip in their section. Alexus had her left hand planted on Bulletface's right knee. There was a lot of diamond jewelry in the VIP Lounge, but none was icier than Blake "Bulletface" King. The world-renowned gangsta rapper wore eight or nine tennis chains with fat white diamonds twinkling all through them. His wrists and fingers were awash with ice. He was like an Egyptian Pharoah seated beside his queen.

"I'm done stripping after tonight," Bunny said, drawing Kitty's attention back to her. "Done doing porn too."

"Yeah?" Kitty Jae touched her straw to her lower lip, but she didn't drink. The tequila was coursing nicely through her veins. "Andy why is that?"

"Just ready to turn the page. Being on *The Real Baddies* has given me opportunities I never even imagined. I can do so much more than what I've been doing, Yesterday afternoon I shot my last scene for Lucid Entertainment. I might do something on my OnlyFans every once in a while, but for now I'm just focused on being better. I got a sex toy line comin' out, a house bein' built from the ground up on the north side, I'm tryna settle down, start me a family. Next dick I suck gon' be my man's.

Kitty Jae came dangerously close to laughing at Bunny's ho philosophy, Only reason she didn't was because she happened to glance at the diamond watch she'd borrowed from Blicky, and looking at it reminded her of the watch that had been taken from her at gunpoint, There was also the idea that her unsympathetic laughter might crush the porn star's dreams, Bunny as a pretty young black woman with reddish brown skin, high cheekbones, and full, pouty lips. She wore her dark brown hair in a French bob, White fishnet stockings gave her thick thighs the appearance of fresh Thanksgiving hams, She had her niece's name, Jayda, inked into the front of her left shoulder in red cursive lettering. The whimsical flare in her light brown eyes said she was smart but willing to play dumb if that's what it took to get along with others.

Instead of laughing, Kitty Jae said, "I got robbed a few hours ago. Behind The Visionary Lounge. They put a gun to my face, took my watch. I 'bout pissed my pants."

Bunny's pouty lips popped open in a gasp. "Whhaaat?" Then she furrowed her brow, squinted her chinky eyes, and closed her mouth for a couple of seconds.. "Wait a minute. I thought The Visionary Lounge was closed. How'd you get robbed over there?""Bankroll Reese let Nya shoot a video in there. I was one of the models. When me and my cousin Tammy came outside to leave, two dusty ass bums hopped out of a beat up Ford Explorer and snatched us up. Walked us behind my G-Wagon.

She sighed, sucked some liquor through her straw, and told Bunny the rest of the story. When she got to the part about the doorman telling her that Tammy might have been involved, Bunny's mouth opened wide again, sans the audible pop.

"So you think she set you up? Your own cousin?"

Kitty nodded. "Seems that way."

"Did you confront her about it?"

"Of course I confronted her. I told her exactly what that man told me, and she said I was crazier than Blicky if I believed that shit. She swore up and down she had never seen them boys before, that the only Rock she know is the one who stay right off Sixteenth and Christiana."

"And what did you say to that?"

Kitty gave a perfunctory shrug and sucked her teeth. "I told her I didn't believe her, called her a two-faced bitch. See, what had happened was, my li'l sister spit right in Tammy's face not even five minutes before we got to the club for that video shoot. Tammy texted somebody right after that happened, and the next thing you know I got a gun in my face. They had all three of us at gunpoint— me, her and the doorman—and yet me and him ended up bein' the only ones who got our shit taken. Ho must think I'm slow or some'n. I put her out right there on Chicago Avenue… and didn't look back."

"That's wild. You gotta be a dirty bitch to set up your own family. I would say I'm surprised, but from what I hear she used to set niggas up for Markio all the time. They say that's how Esco and them other two boys got killed in front of that apartment buildin' she used to stay in on Douglas and Albany. She was s'posed to be givin' Esco some pussy that night." Bunny shook her head, and her eyes wandered over to Prinny's section. She opened her pretty mouth to say something else but hesitated, so that only a tiny sound, the very start of a voiced word, issued forth from her throat.

"Speakin' of Markio," Kitty said, on the last minute of her break, "you see them niggas Prinny got over there with her? Not the one she walked in holdin' hands with, but the other ones." She waited for Bunny to nod and said, "They too lucky they got here after FBS had already left the buildin'"

"I was just about to say that." Bunny's high cheekbones puffed out in a smile. "I was just … about.. to say that."

"They killed my son's uncle, shot him dead as he was standin' next to the ice cream truck with his daughter. D-Mac ain't ever did nothin' to nobody."

Bunny was shaking her head. She let out a sadly despondent "Mm-mm-mm," while Kitty Jae sucked up the last of her tequila.

"Okay," Kitty eased down off the barstool. "let's get this money, Bunny."

Bunny beamed at the rhyme.

Kitty Jae massaged her puffy knuckles, secretly wishing she had a line of coke to numb the ache. She was looking around VIP Louge for a prime spot to dance, imaging herself snorting that gram of powder through a rolled-up dollar bill when she spotted Big Gabby standing in front of Alexus and Bulletface, who were also standing.

All three of them were staring right at Kitty Jae.

Big Gabby pointed an index fingernail at Kitty Jae. Then she swiveled her pudgy brown hand and curled that forefinger again and again, as if she were firing an imaginary pistol at the ceiling.

Kitty Jae lowered her head and started walking.

Chapter 16

"Alexus and Blake would like to hire you for a private dance in the luxury suite," Big Gabby said when the girl with the big tattoo of Micheal Myers on the front of her left thigh made it over to Alexus and Blake's section.

"Okay," Kitty Jae said, "Follow me."

Jason Voorhees was tatted on the dancer's fat left buttock. The entire left side of her body was an artwork of horror movie villains. *Hellraiser, Jeepers Creepers*, Freddy from *Nightmare on Elm Street; Candyman*, the ghost=faced stabber from the Scream movie franchise, the Good Guy doll from *Childs Play*, the sadistic clown from Stephen King's *It*. They were all there, colorfully needled into Kitty Jae's skin from her left ankle all the way up to her left shoulder.

Alexus Costilla-King watched Jason's blood spotted hockey mask as the meaty cheek it was tatted on bounced and jiggled out the stairwell door and across to the hall of VIP Suites. Bojo instructed two of his men to come with them and left the others to guard the men and women they left behind.

The one thing that kept running through Alexus's mind as she and Blake walked behind the bootylicious young stripper was the grim possibility that Princess Kelly might end up arrested and charged for some unsolved murder if Millionaire Markio didn't make it to 54th and Hayne in time to silence the people who knew about it. Alexus couldn't let that happen. Princess was making her way too much money. *The Real Baddies of Chicago* was the most watched reality show on prime-time television. Season One had won an Emmy. *The Real Baddies of St. Louis* would be airing in less than sixty days. Prinny was a glowing-hot star in the entertainment industry, a single black mother whose meteoric rise to stardom was a source of pride and joy for the black community as a whole.

On top of all that, Prinny had essentially grown to become an honorary member of the King Family. She was the first one of Alexus's friends that Blake had ever referred to as his sister, and the kids absolutely adored Prinny's daughter.

There was also the fact that Prinny knew the glaring truth about Alexus and her direct connection to the Matamoros drug cartel. That was something the federal government – and the Trump administration, in particular— had been trying to prove for over a decade.

Blake must have read the hard consternation on his wife's face. He reached over and gave her shoulder a firm, consoling squeeze as they were approaching the Luxury Suite's open door. "It's gon' be a'ight, baby," he said, beaming his diamond smile. "Trump gon' pardon Lil Durk. Just give it some time. Be patient."

"Shut up," Aleus laughed. He always knew what to say. 'I wasn't thinkin' about no Lil Durk.'"Whateva, nigga."

"I wasn't! I swear to God I wasn't." And when Kitty Jae looked back at them with an amused smirk on her face, Alexus sucked a tooth and explained. "He thinks I like Lil Durk more than I like him."

"You should've seen how she watched when he came to the studio last summer. She came in there smilin', offerin' niggas drinks and shit."

"Oh please." Alexus fluttered her eyelashes, "It was a hot day, so I brought in a tray of cold drinks. "

Kitty Jae snickered. "Y'all too funny."

The VIP host was standing outside the door to the Luxury Suite. Her name was Shawnna Wilkins. Alexus could tell the twins apart because she and Blake had done business with their father. They'd sold Juice a thousand bricks of cocaine, and the potbellied man had never looked back.

Shawnna didn't say anything. She merely waved as they passed her, looking abnormally excited just like everyone else Alexus crossed paths with these days. In her heart Alexus was just a country girl from southern Texas, but in the eye of public opinion she was a mogul, one of the most famous women alive. People gasped and stared at her everywhere she went, so Shawnna's stunned reaction was nothing new.

Kitty Jae led Blake and Alexus to the sofa, while Bojo took his signal detector from inside his suit jacket and did a quick walk around the room. He nodded once, gave Alexus an unsmiling thumbs up, and stepped backed out into the hallway, pulling the door shut as he went.

"Was that a metal detector?" Kitty Jae asked.

Pressing her hands down into the sofa's incredibly soft upholstery Alexus wagged her head and said, "No. That was a signal detector. It detects cameras, microphones, cell phones – anything transmitting a signal. Only phone it doesn't' alert to are mine and Blake's.""Oh Wow." Kitty Jae sauntered over and stood in front of Alexus and Blake with her hands splayed on her hips and her head canted slightly to one side. "So – who am I dancing on?"

"No one. " Alexus crossed her legs. "We didn't bring you in here to dance. I wanna know what you're doing dancing to begin with."

Kitty wrinkled her brow. "I don't, I don't understand."

"You just signed a three movie deal with my film company. You're a successful screenwriter. Why are you stripping?"

The defensive shift in Kitty Jae's posture was barely even perceptible; her head moved back on her neck just a few degrees, her eyelids moved maybe one or two centimeters closer together, and her eyes flicked over to Blake before resettling on Alexus.

"I don't know if you read over that contract I signed," she said, "but it didn't include any kind of advance. I actually gave up five hundred thousand dollars."

"I wasn't aware of that. You should've received an advance Who'd you speak with? " Alexus unshouldered her white lambskin Balenciaga purse and took out her iPhone.

It took less than five minutes to rectify the situation. Just three brief phone calls, one text, and a money transfer to Jaresha Brady's checking account.

"Everybody eats," Alexus said, handing her cellphone to Kitty Jae so that the beautiful redbone could see that exactly five million had just been wired to her bank.

Kitty Jae gasped and slapped a hand over her mouth and nose. The eyes above her cupped hand went as wide as they could get. Her knees trembled, making the knife wielding Michael Myers on her left thigh rock left to right.

"No," she said.

"Yes," Alexus replied.

"No, no, no."

"Yes, yes, yes." Alexus got up with her arms outstretched for a hug, and Kitty Jae's arms wrapped around her like two strong octopus tentacles.

Their embrace lasted a long moment. Kitty Jae didn't want to let her go, and Alexus didn't mind at all. She spent the time rubbing her hands up and down Kitty's back, wondering how the exotic dancer would put her newfound wealth to use.

Blake shattered the moment when he started clapping his hands and bobbing his head, showing his diamond coated teeth in the sneaky little half grin that had won his wife's heart over fifteen years ago.

"Yeah. Yeeaah," he said, still nodding and half-grinning. "That's it right there. Baby, you need to move your hands just a little further down her back."

Kitty Jae threw her head back and laughed. Alexus shook her head, rolled her eyes, and smilingly said. "Excuse him. I married a pervert."

"I ain't no pervert. I'm just a street nigga wit' money, sittin' here watchin' two bad, thick-ass bitches hug on each other. How I'm s'posed to react to that? Huh? You think I'ma say some shit you'll hear on one'a dem Hallmark movies or some'n? Hell nah. I'm waitin' on y'all to start kissin'."

"He is too funny," Kitty Jae said, but there was a sparkle in her eye as she handed the phone back to Alexus, and the upward curvature of her lips spoke volumes.

Alexus was feeling it too. She wasn't into women, but there was no denying that Kitty Jae was a true baddie. She was shaped like Saweetie, that California dime who'd rapped her way to fame and fortune. Alexus and Blake had great sex all the time, sometimes three or four sessions in a single day, but lately Alexus had been exploring different ways to spice things up a bit.

A threesome was the ultimate spice.

"You can leave with us, if you want to." Alexus said. She flicked a glance at Blake and saw that he was grinning his approval. "Prinny's feeling a little worried so we're heading over to her place."

Kitty Jae nodded like a Bobblehead, fingering away the joyful tears that had accumulated between her eyelids. "I'm cool with that." She smiled and sniffed. "Shit, I'm *definitely* cool with that. I got five million dollars. Fuck Big Gabby."

The three of them laughed. Kitty Jae left the Luxury Suite to get dressed. Alexus sat across her husband's lap, took his chin in her hand, and kissed him on the mouth.

"You better be lucky I love you like I do," she said.

"I'm gon' fuck the shit outta y'all," was his immediate reply and Alexus knew that he meant every word.

She could hardly wait.

Chapter 17

"She made me do it. She fuckin' *made* me do it. Stupid ass bitch walked right past me, two or three inches from my face, and then she had the nerve to just stop right there, with her fuckin' *back* to me. Like I was some kinda ho or some'n. Like Blicky Motherfuckin' Nicky wasn't about that motherfuckin' action. *Bitch!*

She slammed the side of her fist against the driver window and jumped in her seat when the darkly tinted pane of glass dropped down into the door.

The car was a dark blue Buick Regal that had come from the assembly line sometime in the late 1900's. Blicky had flagged down a nearly toothless old man and offered him all thirty eight of the hundred dollars bills she had in her purse in exchange for his ancient set of wheels.

"And two mo' hun'ed and we got a deal," he'd rasped.

Blicky had wanted to say *Nigga, this piece'a shit ain't worth two dollars*, but she'd seen a pair of police lights flashing three or four blocks away. So she'd added four fifties to the pile of cash and seconds later she'd driven off.

"Wait!" the old man had shouted after her. "My pista! I left my pista in there!"

His *pista* was a blue steel .44 Bulldog revolver with a beige rubber grip. Blicky had found it under the driver seat, and now it lay on the passenger's seat beside her. A gleaming masterpiece of modern weaponry resting on forty-year-old faded yellow vinyl that was so old it had burst open at the seams. Dirty orange foam protruded from the openings like road kill guts.

Blicky Nicky drove her newly acquired brokemoble back to the west side of the city, listening to the steady rattle of the engine and watching out for the police, vaping and occasionally cracking a smile when she thought of how easily she'd defeated Shmoney Rose. She wasn't worried about the police tracking her to her Monticello Avenue home, because the address on her driver's clients was still 6743 South Dorchester Avenue.

Even so, Blicky circled the block twice when she made it home, and trundled through the alleyway once. She parked in front of a neighbor's house and walked hurriedly to her residence, feeling the weight of the Bulldog in her purse. She'd taken it with her because she liked guns, and also because she wanted to believe she'd gotten more than a rusted-out junk of vinyl and steel for her four thousand dollars.

All the first floor lights were on. Light from the living room shone through the pink frill curtains, bathing the concrete porch in a pinkish glow. Blicky could hear Sexyy Red's "Get it Sexyy" blaring from somewhere inside the house. She paused as she used her iPhone to remotely unlock the porch door, wondering what had gotten into her boyfriend, Deshawn Armstead. Shawn was a Black Disciple from 67th and Dorchester, he listened to rap music all day long. But he usually only listened to G Herbo, Lil Durk, King Von and two or three other rappers. The only time Big Sexyy was played in Blicky's house was when she turned it on herself.

"Let this nigga have a bitch in my house," Blicky said under her breath as she stepped into the well-lit, white, vestibule that had once separated the second floor and first floor apartments.

Taking the old man's *pista* out of her gray leather Fendi bag, and feeling that same uncontrollable rage she'd felt just before all hell broke loose in the VIP Lounge, Blicky stalked into the house like a seasoned cat burglar moving along the wall in the short hallway that turned into her living room to keep the floor bards from creaking, walking on the toes of her running shoes as she hurried through the longer hallway that led to the spare bedroom she allowed Zeffy to use whenever she stayed over. She could tell that the music was coming from there. She could also tell, from the clarity of the tunes, that the song was being played through her Alexa speaker.

Blicky made it to the doorway and eased just enough of her head forward to peek one eye into the room.

What she witnessed was so shocking it froze her in place.

Shawn — tall, dark, and the opposite of handsome — lay naked on the bed with his chicken-thin legs drawn back and spread wide. He was jacking his wet dick. Zeffy, also naked was kneeling forward with her head lowered, caressing his balls and licking his asshole. A tube of Astroglide lubricant lay on the Hermes blanket next to Shawn's elbow. The potent stench of exotic marijuana mixed with the mildly fruity smell of the lubricant.

A Cherokee D'Ass porn played on the widescreen TV. Cherokee was face down, ass up on the floor in a spacious living room with white leather sofas all around. The male actor was dunking his huge black Mandingo dick in and out her asshole.

Blicky's tongue pulled away from the roof of her mouth and took her lower jaw with it. She made no effort to soften her footsteps as she moved to stand in the doorway. The sudden rise of her blood pressure made her ears ring as her tremulous forefinger curled in over the Bulldog's trigger.

"My own fuckin' cousin," Blicky said. She shook her head in disbelief.

Zeffy and Shawn's initial reactions were the same: their eyes got big and their heads swung to stare at Blicky as she stood there in the open doorway with the brawny little revolver pointing down by her side.

"Baby!" Shawn said, dropping his legs onto the bed and sitting up. His eyebrows tried to climb up and hide in his dreadlocks, and they almost mader it.

Zeffy demonstrated the fire drill Blicky had learned in her second grade class of elementary school. She stopped, dropped, and rolled off the side of the bed, where she kneeled with only her eyes and forehead showing above the bedside.

"It wasn't me!" Zeffy said. Like that old Shaggy song.

"Then who the fuck was it?" Blicky raised the gun, and Zeffy dipped the rest of her head down beside the gray-blanketed bed. "I swear to God, Zeff, if you don't stand up right fuckin' now…"

Zeffy didn't stand up.

"Bitch, on King David, if you don't stand the fuck up!"

Zeffy popped up like a slice of bread from a toaster, holding one arm across her chest and the other hand over her clean shaven pussy. She was leaner than Blicky, longer in the limbs and pretty. She didn't have much in the hips, but her ass was fat and round like Blicky's, and she had sexy brown eyes.

Eyes that were now fearful and brimming with tears.

"Nasty bitch. Fuckin' ass eater." Blicky turned to scowl at her boyfriend. He had just covered his crotch with a pillow. "How long this shit been goin' on? How long you been fuckin' my cousin? And since when you start lettin' bitches play in you' bootyhole?"

"Baby, put the gun down.""I should blow your dick off."

"Put the gun down," Shawn repeated, more sternly than before.

Blicky took aim at the cock-blocking pillow. "Say that again. I triple-dog dare you. Say it just one more motherfuckin' time and see what I do. Go ahead. You brave. You Mr. Billy Badass. Go ahead and say it."

Shawn didn't say it. He didn't utter a single word. His eyes blinked. His flat, hairless chest rose and fell. He pulled the center of the silk pillowcase into his hand and balled it in his fist. Flexed his toes.

The spell was broken when Zeffy bent down to pick up her red lace panties. Blicky's teeth clashed together, and her arm swung over to aim at Zeffy's chest.

"Bitch, did I tell you to move?"

"I'm not about to stand her butt-ass naked," Zeffy said, stepping into her panties. "You need to put that gun down so we can talk about this like adults."

"Didn't I just tell him not to say that?" Blicky Nicky brought her other hand up to hold the heavy revolver the way it was meant to be held. "You must think it's a game. You must think I'm a joke. Okay. Okay. Okay, ho."

Zephyra Estrada was bending over and reaching for the red lace bra that was hanging down off the corner of the bed when Blicky folded her lips in over her teeth, bit down, and squeezed the trigger.

The blast was deafening.

Blicky nearly lost her grip on the pistol as it bucked in her hand. The bullet grooved the side of Zeffy's head, blowing her hair back and sending a spray of blood onto her bare shoulder. She snapped to attention and clamped her hand to the superficial graze wound on the side of her head, her mouth stretched wide in a gasp of horror.

"You think it's a game!" Blicky screamed. *"You think I ain't about that motherfuckin' action!"*

She took careful aim and fired again. This time she had a firmer grip on the pistol, and the .44 caliber slug cut a perfect hole in the middle of Zeffy's upper lip. The impact threw Zeffy's back against the smooth white wall. Her brains splashed against the wall behind her as if the back of her skull had a mouth and vomited them out.

Shawn leapt off the bed and reached Blicky in a single stride. He twisted her wrist with one hand and wrested the gun from her with the other. Not that she put up much of a fight. She was far too mesmerized by the cranial sludge that was slowly oozing down the wall toward Zeffy lifeless body.

"Look at what the fuck you just did!" Shawn exclaimed.

"Shot that ho in the lip!" Blicky smiled widely and let out a single yip of laughter. Electric energy crackled through her every vein. She looked over at Shawn as he let go of her wrist. "Put on some clothes," she said, gently rubbing her hand up and down his naked hip. "We need to get gone before the police get here. They're kinda lookin' for me right now."

Shawn dressed in a hurry – no underwear, no socks, just a green pair of Amiri sweatpants, the sweatshirt that went with it, green-and-white '95 Air Max sneakers, and nothing else. He kept the gun in his hand and an eye on Blicky the whole time, but she hardly even noticed.

"Look at those *brains*," she said. "Looks like I shattered a jar of Ragu sauce against that wall, don't it."

"Man, you crazy." Shawn said, in fluctuating tones of stunned realization. "You are really fuckin' crazy."

"Crazy about you." She cheesed and made her eyebrows jump "Come on. I got the perfect getaway car. Wait until you see the brokemobile I just bought."

Chapter 18

"Shmoney's pressing charges."

"I'm not surprised."

"Neither am I. It took seven staples and twelve stitches to close that gash in the back of her head. They had to shave a lot of her hair off back there. We're staked out here in the parking lot outside of Northwestern Memorial, just me and a couple of others, two cameramen. We still have five camera persons at Queen of Diamonds, and I sent Mike over to Blicky's house in case she shows up there. He's— hold on, this is him on the other line."

The FaceTime video stream on *The Real Baddies of Chicago*'s lead field producer, Robyn Jarrett, blanked out on Prinny's phone screen, so she set the phone down on her thigh and sucked smoke from the blunt of Black Cherry Gelato her bestie Asia had rolled for her hours earlier. She closed her eyes as she toked, relishing the low sizzle of the ember burning away at the buds. She felt sexy, safe and comfortable with her surgical fattened butt resting on Zoodie's lap and his arm draped casually around her waist.

There were nine of them seated on the sumptuous Italian leather sofas in the cavernous living room of Prinny's Highland Park mansion. Alexus and her rap superstar husband were two of them. The other were Nishelle and her boyfriend, Keith "Keymo" Cox; Nya "YoungNya" Mixon and her man, Demetruis "Young Meach" Burns; Nya's best friend, Noesha Long, who was just as green-eyed, curvy and beautiful as Alexus Costila; and Jaresha "Kitty Jae" Brady.

Beyonce's "Drunk In Love" video was playing on the massive television screen. Prinny had dimmed the lights. They had arrived just thirty minutes prior and they were already settled in.

Chill vibes permeated the room.

Everyone had gone silent to listen to Prinny's FaceTime call with the field producer.

When Robyn's head and the headrest behind it reappeared on Prinny's phone screen a moment later, she looked grim. Her thumb-shaped face had taken on the stunned expression of someone who had just witnessed a severe tragedy.

"You are not going to believe this," Robyn said.

"Try me," Prinny challenged, exhaling a great plume of smoke toward the high ceiling.

"Okay, so I told you I sent our cameraman Mike over to Blicky's place," Robyn began, "Well, when he got there, he found the place crawling with police. He couldn't even get close to the building, but he did get a chance to speak with the neighbor who reported the shooting. She said she was awakened by two loud gunshots. By the time she got to her front window to look out and see what was going on, the man with the gun was running up the sidewalk on Blicky's side of the street. She said it was Blickey's boyfriend, said he was wearing green pants and a green sweatshirt and that he got in the passenger's side of an old blue two-door before it went speeding away. She thinks whoever was driving must have made it into the car just before the boyfriend did, because she heard a car door slam two or three seconds before she made it to the window."

"So what happened?" Alexus asked from two seats down. "Is Blicky okay? Was somebody shot?"

Prinny knew what Quenen A was thinking. She wasn't in any way concerned about Blicky Nicky's true well-being.

150

She just didn't want the psycho to die, because Blicky Nicky was a ratings magnet.

"Oh, it's worse than that," Robyn said, "Somebody was *killed*. Mike doesn't think it was Blicky, because he asked one of the cops if there was a purple rose tattooed behind the victim's left ear, and the cop said there wasn't. Were guessing it's her cousin."

"Zeffy," Kitty Jae said. She was on the sofa that faced the one Prinny was on. Nya and Noesha, her fellow West Siders, were seated to her left and right.

"Yeah," Robyn nodded. "Zeffy. She's always there when we're filming. She'd serve drinks and snacks to the crew, wipe down the tables, that sort of thing."

Prinny scrubbed a hand down her face. "I'm too high for this shit," she said, truly meaning it. She was already worried over the situation with Sadé and Tramell. One of her most popular cast members was now in the hospital with seven staples in the back of her head. Prinny just couldn't take any more drama. "We've got more than enough footage for tonight. You all can go home. And tell Mike to get from over there before he gets himself shot.".

Hearty chuckles were beginning to spread around the living room as Princess ended the video call.

"I'm too high for this shit," Nya mocked. Short and pretty, she had the same reddish-brown complexion that Kitty Jea had. The white diamond PLUSH GANG pendant that hung from her Cuban link chain was so large that Prinny really believed Nya's claim that it had cost her $400,000.

Prinny ignored Nya's lighthearted echo of a joke to address Kitty Jae.

"Will you please call your friend and let me talk to her?" It came out more like a defeated plea than a question.

Kitty Jae, who hadn't stopped smiling since they left the club, showed a few more of her teeth and said, "My movie gon' be a blockbuster. Watch. Y'all just watch." Bobbing her head up and down, she raised her phone and dialed a number, presumably Blicky's.

"I hope Blicky's okay," Alexus said, her Colgate commercial smile directed at Kitty Jae, "Bonding her out of jail for what happened at the club is one thing, but murder is something totally different. Hopefully she wasn't the getaway driver."

"She that crazy." Nishelle asked.

"I'm her only friend," Kitty Jae said, as her smartphone rang in the palm of her open hand. "Trust me when I tell you this: Blicky is way more fucked up in the head than you could possibly imagine. Like, she unlocked a whole new secret level of crazy. I'm not saying she would go against her own cousin, but I'm not saying she wouldn't either. You never really know with Blicky. If she feels slighted in any way she'll be out for revenge until she gets it."

"Sounds like my kinda bitch," Nya said.

"I was about to say the same thing," Alexus said, nodding her braided head.

Prinny tapped her blunt over the Louis Vuitton saucer she used as an ashtray. Seconds later, Nishelle complained that the dim lighting was dimming her mood, so Prinny got up, crossed the room to the touchscreen lighting controls, and brightened the lights.

She flinched when she saw that there was a tenth person in the living room.

Bojo was standing in one corner with his big arms crossed over his brawny chest, his head titled forward, and his uniquely vigilant eyes fixed on Prinny. His thick bottom lip stuck out in front of the top one, nearly swallowing it up. The twenty Mexican men he employed to help him keep Alexus safe were out in Prinny's 3,200-square-foot guest house. Bojo had led them out there, but Prinny hadn't sent him return. He must have been standing there in the shadows for some time, his smooth white suit camouflaging him against the smooth white wall behind him.

Nishelle fetched the Hennessy and poured drinks for everyone but Meach and Bulletface, who only drank Lean. The liquor loosened their tongues, and soon there was laughter and conversation all around. Kitty Jae made a few more calls to Blicky Nicky, but she kept getting sent to voicemail. So she pursed her phone and spent ten minutes regaling the room with the story outline to her upcoming horror flick. Nya and Meach said they wanted in on the movie soundtrack, which then turned into Nya recounting the time she and her friend Lacey had visited a haunted house somewhere out in Bronzeville. Lacey let a zombie and an axe-wielding clown run a train on her in the bed of a pickup truck, and the taste of the zombie's cum had made her puke.

Sipping her drink and enjoying the subtle weight of Zoodie's hand on her thigh, Prinny listened closely as Nya spoke about her old friend Lacey. Prinny remembered when, just a couple years ago, all the local news channels had been replete with stories about the mysterious disappearance of Lacey Carter. She was last seen leaving out of the emergency room doors of a Chicago hospital, pushing Nya in a wheelchair and surrounded by a few other member of their Plush Gang sisterhood. After helping Nya – who'd been shot in the leg – into one of their two SUV's, the girls had driven away.

Lacey Carter was never seen or heard from again.

Prinny considered asking Nya and Noesha what they believed happened to Lacey. She opened her motu and drew in a light breath to voice the question. but then she remembers one of the many wild conspiracy theory that had sprouted up on social media int eh wake of Lacey's disappearance, the one that pointed out how Nya and her girl had started hanging out with Alexus right around the time Lacey went missing, and that Alexus had started rocking a PLUSH GANG chain that looked remarkably similar to the one Lacey was last seen wearing.

Which brought Prinny back to the question she'd asked Alexus in the VIP Lounge a few hours ago, and the cryptic answer Alexus had given her:

"The old man Herb Is he gone for good? I mean, where is he?"

Alexus had answered, "He's with Whitney Clarrett," and then she'd flashed her frigid-eyed smile.

Whitney Clarrett was the founder of iKiss Kosmetics, a successful line of lip gloss, lipstick, and other cosmetics that had carved out its own little niche in the multi-billion dollar makeup industry. Whitney was also Millionaire Mrkio's ex-girlfriend. She and a group of friends had gone out partying at Redbone's Gentleman's Club— a strip club in North Lawndale that just so happened to be owned by Markio's cousin, Bankroll Reese— and upon leaving she'd been snatched into a stolen SUV at gunpoint and taken.

Whitney Clarrett was never seen or heard from again.

The striking similarities between Whitney and Lacey's sudden and unexpected disappearances, and their salient connections to Alexus Costilla, made Princess swallow the question she had about Lacey Carter.

Kitty Jae stood up and asked for directions to the bathroom. At the same time, Alexus whispered something in her husband's ear, and they both got up from the sofa.

"I need to go too," Alexus said to Prinny.

"Y'all follow me," Prinny said, leading Alexus and Kitty Jae out of the living room. She heard Bulletface tell Zoodie to come on and knew right then something was up.

Her gut instinct told her it was something good.

Chapter 19

"I can't believe you actually did that shit. You shot your own goddam cousin. Shot her in the face. What the fuck."

"No, no, no. No, no, no, no, no. Damn that. Let's talk about how that bitch had her tongue in your motherfuckin' ass. Let's talk about *that*."

"She's dead, Blicky. She ain't comin' back."

Blicky turned and looked at Shawn like he was crazy before turning her eyes back to the road ahead. "You think I'm slow or some'n? I know what the fuck *dead* mean. You lucky you grabbed that gun out my hand when you did. Ever heard of Sleepless in *Seattle*? Yo' motherfuckin' ass would've been *Brainless in Chicago*. Bitch."

Shawn had nothing to say to that. He shook his dreads and stared at the broken glove compartment in front of him. Its door hung down like the jaw of a panting canine.

They had taken Central Avenue to Interstate-290 and got off on Congress Parkway. After that Blicky had found a nice little hideout behind a house near Minister Rico's convenience store on 16th Street and Lawndale Avenue, and there they'd sat for the better part of an hour, Shawn smoking his Newport's, Blicky vaping while watching the police search through her house from her security cameras, which she accessed through an app on her iPhone.

The Police One app had been equally helpful. It told her what the cops were broadcasting over their police radio scanners. At first there was an All-Points Bulletin for a dark-colored older model car, possibly a Buick or Oldsmobile.

Twenty minutes later the APB was updated to a much more spot-on description: A dark blue or purple Buick Regal, late 1980's model, license plate CXL64256, last seen on traffic camera going southbound on Central Avenue.

They had sat there behind that stranger's house, wedged between an old brown Chevy van and another van that might have been that old van's great-grandson, hidden next to a big leafless tree with a huge rubber truck tire suspended from a braided yellow rope that was tied around its thickest branch. There was a cat perched inside the tire with only its jet-black head sticking up out of it. Blicky had used the screwdriver she'd seen on the floor behind Shawn's feet to steal the newborn van's license plate and put it on the Regal; the black cat had watched her so closely as she changed the license plates that she'd turned to it and hissed like a vampire.

Now she was back on the road, going east on 16th Street. She clicked her vape pen, filled her lungs with smoke, and contemplated snatching the gun out of Shawn's hand. Or at least attempting to.

"How long you and her been fuckin'?" She asked the question without looking at him. "Hm? How long?"

"Do it even matter?" Shawn replied, answering her question with one of his own.

"Yes, it does. It does matter. You sick fuck. And what the fuck was *you* on at Dixon Correctional Center? You didn't like no tongue in yo' ass before you *went* to prison. Now you come home and you Rick James. Let me find out..."

"You got me fucked up. On Lil Steve, don't even play wit' me like that. That was yo' freaky-ass cousin who wanted to do that shit. I let that bitch suck my dick a few times, and she kept wantin' to eat my ass, so I let her eat my ass."

"That's 'cause you gay."

"Fuck outta here. Ain't shit fruity about me. I was in *heavy* rotation with the Folks at Dixon, at Menard, *and* at Stateville. Ain't neva had no fag shit on my name. Got me fucked up. I should slap yo' stupid ass for even sayin' some—"

Shawn stopped talking mid-threat because Blicky pressed her foot down hard on the gas pedal. She reached up over her shoulder and pulled her seatbelt down across her chest. Her malevolent scowl became a benevolent smile when she heard the distinctive click of the belt securing itself in the buckle.

"You should do what now?"

"Man, what the fuck is wrong witchoo? Slow dis muhfucka down!"

"*You're* what's wrong with me."

Blicky swerved around a dirty white Pontiac Grand Am and came within inches of side-wiping its driver's side. The young black woman in the driver seat flinched away from her door and gawked at the Regal as it rocketed past.

The plan had been to drive down to Kitty Jae's house on 16th and Millard and get her boyfriend, Two Ton, to let them borrow his Tahoe. Then they could jump on the highway and head down to Orange County, Florida, where Blicky's uncle Fernando owned a house in the gated Wintermere Pointe subdivision.

"Change'a plans, Freaky Shawn!" Blicky's smile belonged on the face of a ghoulishly sinister Halloween mask.

The Buick streaked right past Millard Avenue. Six or seven black teenage boys were walking past Dvorak High School. Blicky heard one of them yelling. "Rocks, Weed, Blows!" as she sped by, and a few of his friends cringed and reached for their waistlines, likely fearing the Regal might be occupied by rival gang members.

Traffic on 16th Street was light for a Friday night. Only two more vehicles were swerved around before Blicky got the speedometer up to sixty miles per hour

Stricken with panic in the passenger's seat, Shawn went through a number of precautionary measures. His first move was to raise the Bulldog and aim it at the side of Blicky's maniacally smiling head. "Bitch, I sweah to God…," he said, and then he grabbed the dashboard and expelled a fart that sounded wet and squishy in his pants. Next, he tried yanking down his own seatbelt, but it wouldn't budge from over his shoulder.

"For God so loved the world," Blicky said, stomping the pedal to the floor, "that he gave his only begotten Daugther, that whosever goeth against her shall *perish the everlasting fire.*!"

She screamed the last five words as she veered over into the westbound lane… right into the path of an oncoming SUV.

Chapter 20

Only the upstairs lights at the rear of 5358 South Hoyne Avenue were on when the light gray Dodge Durango SRT Hellcat came rumbling to a stop in the alleyway behind it. An old Gucci Mane song, "Choppa Shoppin," pulsed from inside the SUV, and when Markio, the driver, reached for the center console to kill the music, the only sounds to be heard were the hollow whistles of wind blowing through the fenced-in yards and the melodious tunes of Tyrese's "Sweet Lady" playing in the backyard two houses down.

A dog unleashed a serios of loud, vicious-sounding barks from somewhere behind the Durango.

"I say we just walk down there and nail buddy," Baby Lord suggested form his seat behind Markio. His words were slightly muffled from the mask he wore over his dark black face. It covered everything but his eyes. "Catch his ass lackin' on some slow-dance shit, turn that li'l R and B party to a drill party."

"Nah," Markio said. "Just be patient. Too many people down there right now. I ain't tryna hit no bystanders."

"Man, fuck them niggas. These niggas ova here snitched on Bo. He got booked for a double murda right here on this block. Everybody who seen it told."

Markio didn't know many people this far south, so he didn't speak on the allegations. He was only here because he owed eleven million dollars to the Matamoros drug cartel, and Queen A had offered to slice that debt in half once he neutralized the threats to Prinny's freedom. He'd chosen

Baby Lord to accompany him on the mission because Baby Lord was fast on his feet and really good at killing people. It was also rumored that Baby Lord was somewhat of a good luck charm when it came to murder missions. He was the hitman who always go away. He'd been arrested for murder just once, and he'd beat that case at trial just six months after Markio and another high-ranking TVL called Bam had bailed him out for a million in cash.

"You still ain't told me what I'm gettin' paid," Baby Lord said. He always spoke rapidly, as if someone had activated a fast-forward switch in his voice box. "You ain't told me who this nigga is, where he came from, what he did— nothin'. Nothin' but this screenshot."

"He's a rat," Markio said. He'd smoothed his mask out on his armrest, and now he just sat with one leather-gloved forefinger hooked over the lower curvature of his steering wheel and his unwavering gaze on the tall wooden fence two houses north of Sadé and Tramell's place. "Him and his girl know some'n about a body. That body cold get somebody who's really important locked up."

"I knew it had to be somebody important for you to get involved. You could've easily just sent the gang. Shit, me and Gucci Ball could've slid over here and whacked buddy."

Markio nodded his head a couple of times and kept on staring.

He'd changed out of his club attire after he dropped Apple off at his Spaulding Avenue home. Now he wore a plain black Dollar Store hoodie over equally cheap black sweatpants and black Air Force 1's. The .45-caliber Glock 50 resting on his left thigh had a 50-shot drum magazine and was modified to fire like a machine gun. He'd left his business phone at the North Lawndale home he'd purchased early last year— a three-story redbrick building on the 1600 block of Drake Avenue— but he'd kept the prepaid phone he used to conduct his more illicit affairs.

Millionaire Markio had a sprawling drug empire that spanned nine states and employed hundreds of street-level dealers in trap houses, seedy motel rooms, and affordable housing complexes all across the great U.S. of A. Upper-echelon members of his Fin Ball Shortiez gang would take delivery of his drug shipments from the Matamoros drug cartel, deliveries that usually took place inside abandoned warehouses or rural Airbnb mansions, and those shipments – normally consisting of at least one or two thousand kilograms of pure Colombian cocaine, a few hundred kilos of Mexican heroin, and five or six thousand pounds of exotic marijuana and Mexican made "super meth" – were then distributed to other high level dealers. Some of them were in his FBS squad, but most were in other Chicago neighborhoods, and a few dozen were in other cities and states. It was an immensely lucrative operation that brought in a lot more cash than he could spend, roughly a million dollars every day, all thanks to Alexus Costilla and the Mexican drug cartel hardly anyone knew she ran.

Despite his unyielding loyalty to Alexus, Markio knew the real reason why he was sitting here in this relatively dark Hoyne Avenue alleyway with a gun in his lap and a mask on his knee. It was his heart wrenching love for Princess Kelly that had brought him here. Seeing her walk into QOD's VIP Lounge holding hands with another man had taken him on a rollercoaster ride of emotions that superseded every bit of intellect he possessed. A warm sensation of pure bliss had washed over him when he first laid eyes on her, but that perfect joy was replaced by a startled look of confusion when he saw that she and the tall burly, Jamaican-looking man who'd walked in behind her were holding hands.

The emotion that came after that was cold, dark, and sinister, like the south side alleyway Markio and Baby Lord were sitting in. That emotion was an explosive combination of jealousy and rage.

He'd wanted to kill that Jamaican-looking man.

"Bro. Look." Baby Lord's sleeved arm lanced forward over Markio's right shoulder, the forefinger at the end of it extended and pointing. "They comin' out."

The eight-foot wooden gate in the equally tall fence that bordered the backyard two houses down had sprung open. Seven or eight partygoers, most of them young black women, spilled out into the alleyway. Markio had been watching for the gate to open, but he'd been so lost in his own thoughts that he didn't see the people until Baby Lord pointed them out.

By then two of the girls were walking toward the Durango, talking loud enough for Markio to hear, while the others stayed back and watched.

"Man, they walkin' towards us," Baby Lord said, pulling off his mask and dipping back in his seat as he spoke.

One of the approaching girls was saying, "Tramell just scary. He been like that forever."

"That nigga be high on that shit! That's what is.," said her friend.

They were dressed the same, in skintight leggings, Air Max '97 sneakers, and light jackets over fitted sweaters. The girl who said Tramell was scary was light-skinned and pretty in the face with a head that was longer than it was wide. Her hair was tied back in a ponytail that swung side to side as she walked. Her jacket was blue. The girl in the brown jacket was thicker and just as pretty. Her hair was mostly hidden beneath a brown Chicago Bulls fitted cap, the bill of which concealed her gorgeous features as she bowed her head to peer in at the contents of her blue plastic cup.

Markio, stuck the gun down between his door and his seat, slipped the mask under his thigh, and forced a smile as he lowered his darkly tinted window. The wind blew a flirtatious stream of cold in his face.

"S'cuse me," said the girl in the blue jacket. The whites of her eyes were about as red as her lipstick. "I know this gon' sound crazy, but are you here to kill somebody name Tramell?"

"Huh?" It was all Markio could manage.

She took his huh as negation. "See? See what I'm sayin', cuzzo?" Her ponytail was a slavemaster's whip, lashing her right shoulder as she spun her head to the left to look at her cousin. "That nigga was high out his mind. Done took that girl car and sped off like that. He ought'a be ashamed'a his self." Her whip came down on the opposite shoulder as she turned back to Markio's window and explained. "This nigga named Tramell just tweaked hard on us. He my girl Sadé's baby daddy or whatever, and the nigga tweaked the fuck out when you pulled up back here. He was already swearin' up and down that Princess Kelly – the bitch who made that TV show, *The Real Baddies of Chicago* –mn was gon' send some Stones ova her to kill him. I guess Sadé used to kick it wit' Princess, and Princess came over to see her while Tramell was at that sandwich shop, and for whatever reason he took that as a sign that she was gon' send some niggas ova her to kill him and maybe even her."

Ducked low in the seat behind Markio, Baby Lord whispered, "Man, what the fuck?" Or maybe that wasn't Baby Lord. Maybe that was a product of Markio's own imagination. It certainly aligned with what he was thinking.

"The nigga got a camera on Sadé's roof that looks right down into this alley." The girl with the red eyes continued. "He had been watchin' from his phone when you pulled up a few minutes ago. That's when he really tweaked. He grabbed Sadé by the arm and ran through the gangway on the side of our house. One of our friends had just pulled up out front. Tramell gave her a hundred dollars to use her car for an hour, and he sped off with Sadé.

The other girl said, "Where he get that hun'ed dollars from though? That's what I wanna know. It was a brand new hun'ed too. That boy ain't' never had more than forty dollars to his name."

She stepped up beside her cousin and stared in at Markio. Her brow wrinkled and then her eyes got big. She backhanded her red-eyed cousin's shoulder half a dozen times and said "Girl that's … that's…" She snapped her fingers five times. "Bulletface name-dropped him in that song we don't like! He wrote that movie that got Taraji and Micheal B. Jordan in it!"

"Millionaire Markio?" Red Eyes copied Bulls Hat's expression, furrowing her brow and then opening her eyes full-mast as she leaned in to get a better look at the man to whom she was speaking. She gasped and brought her hand up to cover her gaping mouth. *"Millionaire Markio!* Oh my God that *is* you! I read some of your books! Oh my God, can I get a picture for my Insta? I fuckin' hate Vice Lords, but I love me some you!"

"Bitch," Baby Lord muttered from the backseat, and that time Markio knew for sure it was him.

The girl in the Bulls hat waved her friend over, shouting, "Y'all, come look! It's Millionaire Markio!"

Markio emitted a dry chuckle and shook his head in disbelief as the people came running.

Chapter 21

"What are you still doing woke? It's almost one o'clock."

Eleven-year-old Omar Kyrie McCullough Jr. bared his teeth in a sleepy smile that warmed Kitty Jae's heart. His handsome brown visage filled the screen of her iPhone. He was in bed, lying on his side with his head turned in a way that kept the side of his face from sinking into his pillow.

"I got woke up by the car crash," he said.

"Car crash? What car crash."

"Somebody just crashed into a truck on Sixteenth Street. Grandma walked down to the corner and looked. She said it's a really bad accident. A man was ejected from the car. They say he flew right through the windshield and landed on the sidewalk twenty feet away. Some girl crawled out of the car with blood all over her, screaming that the man had kidnapped her and hot somebody at her house," He blew air through his lips. People are crazy."

"Did the man die?"

"Mmm-hhmm. That's what they told Grandma. She didn't walk all the way down there. But she could see his body from the corner. They say his pants was halfway down and he wasn't wearin' no underwear."

"Damn," Kitty Jae said, and for a moment she and her son giggled like immature schoolchildren.

She was standing in the middle of a bathroom that was roughly the side of her living room. The glassed-in shower directly ahead of her was all marble on the inside, and there was a television built into the wall beside the marble bench.

She'd only had to pee, but she'd use the bidet afterward just because she'd never used one before.

Sometime during their giggling fit, in a part of her brain that was only partially active, a connection was made between the conversation she'd overheard Prinny having with the field producer and the news her son had just broke to her about the 16th Street car crash, but she was either too drunk or too happy to see it for what it was.

"Before you go to sleep," she said, "text four of your friends and see if their parents will agree to let them fly out of state with us this upcoming weekend."

"Fly out of *state!*" OJ sat up in bed, beaming. It was almost as if an invisible baby had sat on his head and yanked him up by the eyebrows. "Fly out of state! Where? Where, Mama. Where are we flying to? You better not say what I'm thinking."

"You better not scream."

"Disney World?"

"Disney World,"

OJ threw his head back and yowled like an injured cartoon villain. He sprang to his feet and jumped up and down in his bed. He offered his laughing mother a series of repeated thank yous, impervious to her request for him to quiet down.

"Go to sleep, Omar. We're going shopping tomorrow, and I don't want you getting all sleepy on me while I'm trying on clothes. You know I like to take my time."

"Don't I know it." He rolled his eyes and fell back onto his pillow. "I don't know how I'm gonna get any sleep, though. I'm so turnt up right now I can't even think straight."

Kitty eyes went up in the start of an eyeroll that never quite made it to the finish line. "Bye, boy," she said and ended the call.

After that she went to her banking app and spent a long, quiet, happy moment staring at her checking account balance. *$4,957,884.29*. The transfer was electronically approved about an hour after Alexus sent it, with the current balance reflecting the cash Kitty had left after having allowed her bank to deduct the remaining $71,599.20 she'd owed for a business loan.

She'd started her day with a little over twenty-nine grand in her checking account, and now she was a certified millionaire.

A *multi*millionaire.

"God is so good," she said, heaving a great, wonderful sigh of relief that seemed to drop all the weight of the world from her shoulders. "Won't He do it. Won't He *do it.*"

She willed herself not to cry but a trickle of salty emotion seeped out of her tear ducts anyway. She sniffed a couple of times and used one cutely manicured thumbnail to gently scrape the moisture away from her eyes. Then she took in a deep nasal breath, let it out in an exhale that sounded like a sigh, and walked to the door. The bits of information she'd taken from Prinny's conversation with Robyn Jareett and Omar's description of the female car crash victim came together in her head to form something a lot more solid as she reached out for the doorknob, and when she pulled the door open and saw Alexus Costilla standing there in the adjoining guest bedroom, laughing with Prinny about something while Bulletface and the Haitian man sat on the huge California King bed and stared at their women, the completed thought rolled to the front of her mind and dropped down onto her tongue like a bag of potato chips in a vending machine.

"I'm pretty sure Blicky just got in a car accident on Sixteenth Street," Kitty Jae said, "And I think her boyfriend, Shawn, might be dead."

Queen A's mirthful disposition switched to a much more devious mien. So did Prinny's. The scary Mexican giant was nowhere in sight, but Kitty Jae saw two narrow shadows in the light that spilled in under the closed bedroom door, and she figured those narrow shadows were cast by Bojo's oversized feet.

Still holding her phone, Kitty tapped into Facebook and swiped through her news feed in search of any video her neighborhood friends might have posted of the accident. She found what she was looking for almost immediately. Brian Dorsey, who called himself Moncler OFF the Ana, had streamed the video. Kitty had gone to North Lawndale College Prep High school with him and his sisters. Principal Nicole Howard had expelled him from school in his sophomore year after catching him with a loaded handgun in his backpack.

Brian's video began as he and a group of younger boys-= all of them reputed gang members; Traveling Vice Lords and Four Corner Hustlers – walked east on 16th Street. The camera was aimed at the crash site: a dark blue Buick Regal with a horribly mangled front end and a white Lexus SUV that had been hit so hard in the collision that its front driver's side tire was knocked hallway down the street.

Kitty Jae waved Alexus and Prinny over and showed them the video, restarting it so all three of them could watch from the beginning. Bulletface and the Haitian man got up and stood behind them just as the Buick's female driver was shoving open the driver door and crawling out on her bloodied hands. The hood of the woman's hoodie dropped down over her dripping head as she crawled out onto the street, but Kitty Jae knew it was Blicky. The gray and blue OTF hoodie was among Blicky's most favored articles of clothing. It had a photo of a smiling Lil Durk on the back with *Free Mr. Banks* inscribed below it in gray cursive lettering.

"That's definitely Blicky," Prinny said.

The camera went all shaky as Brian helped Blicky to her feet and hustled her away from the smoking wreckage. He got her to the sidewalk at the northeast corner of 16th Street and St. Louis Avenue, and she laid down on her back. Her nose looked broken. Her pretty face was powdered from the deployed air bag, and there was blood on her nose, mouth and teeth. She kept grimacing and rubbing her neck with hands that glittered with shattered glass.

"Damn, shorty," Brian said. "Why you speed up like that? I might be tweakin' but it looked like you did that shit on purpose."

"He kidnapped me. He, he killed my cousin." Blicky turned her head and spat a mouthful of blood on the sidewalk. A tooth came out with it. "He shot Zeffy… in the face… and then, and then he made me… made me leave with him."

In between gasps and grimaces, while someone in the background made a call to nine one one, Blicky gave Brain a few more details about her relative's murder. Shawn had apparently been having an affair with Zeffy for some time. Having returned home from QOD earlier than usual, Blicky had walked in on them as they were naked and arguing. Shawn was mad that Zeffy had slipped her tongue into his butthole when she was down there sucking his balls.

"She said…" Blicky coughed and winced and smiled with wet red teeth ".. she said, 'You liked it, you sugar tank butt bandit,' and that's when he, that's when he shot her."

Kitty Jae knew right then that Blicky was lying through her bloody teeth. She'd been around Zeffy enough times to know that the girl would fuck a dog if you left her around it long enough, but Zeffy was no jokester. It was Blicky who'd garnered a sizable social media following for being the undisputed queen of colorful insults. Calling someone a sugar tank butt bandit' was right up her alley.

Kitty found it incredibly difficult to focus on the video with Bulletface standing so close behind her. The faint breeze of his breath on the nape of her neck sent chills through her entire body, from the top of her head to the soles of her feet. His scent, a fragrant combination of cologne, Lean, weed smoke and the natural smell of a man was so alluring that Kitty closed her eyes and flared her nose to take it all in, without even realizing she was doing it.

Jaresha Brady was madly in love with Bulletface.

She'd watched every single one of his music videos, not just the ones that were his songs but also the ones he was featured in. She'd gone to at least one show on every single one of his concert tours, and she could recite every song word for word. Back in the days when she and her friends were all high school teenagers, they would see his lime green Bugatti go slicing past on 16th Street, usually followed by a dazzling fleet of lime green Lamborghinis, Ferraris, and Rolls Royce's, and they would take off running after him. Whenever they were lucky enough to get close to where he'd parked, he would give them money, let them hug and take pictured with him, and he'd usually send them off with a signed copy of his latest album or some piece of merchandise they could show off to their friends at school.

There were only four heads on her mount Rushmore of rap great's— Drake, Future, Lil Durk and Bulletface— and Bulletface's thuggishly handsome countenance was right there at the forefront.

"I'll bond her out," Alexus was saying when Kitty Jae's eyes fluttered open. "They're gonna arrest her when she gets to the hospital, and they might even try charging her as an accomplice to her cousin's murder, but I'll send my lawyer to have a talk with the prosecutor. She'll be out by noon."

"I don't buy that story she's selling," Prinny said. "I mean it's plausible, but I don't believe she went from being a madwoman at Queen of Diamonds to being an innocent victim when she got home. There's more to the story than that"

"Maybe so," Alexus said. She stepped in between her hubby and the woman who was lusting over his scent. Her arms eased in around Kitty Jae's waist, and she brought her chin to rest on Kitty's right shoulder. "But it's the story we're going with. Not about to sit back and allow the police to just take away one of MTN's biggest assets."

Kitty Jae exited Facebook to her iPhone's home screen and then shut the screen off altogether. Her skin was tingling with excitement. Being hugged from behind by Alexus Costilla was no different than being hugged from behind by Beyouncé Knowles, or Mariah Carey, or God Himself. It was a moment of magic, the impossible made possible, a real once-in-a-lifetime experience.

All Kitty Jae could do was smile.

"Question," Alexus said in a voice so low that her words could only be meant for the woman whose ear was two inches away from her mouth. "If I let you fuck my husband, you won't lawyer up on us five years from now and cry rape, will you?"

"I am not that kinda bitch," Kitty said.

"Good. Good." Alexus nodded her chin on Kitty's shoulder. I believe you. Blake and I, we looked at your Instagram on the way here. You came across as a solid kinda bitch." Her hands moved slowly up the front of Kitty's black Louis Vuitton sweater and landed on her breasts, where they paused for a breathtaking squeeze. Finally she took Kitty by the elbow and turned her around.

Which was when Kitty saw that the passion had already ignited between Princess and her a Haitian man. The two of them were locked in a fiery kiss. He was rubbing his hands up and down the perfectly spherical slopes of her ass while she held him by the neck and sucked his lips with hers.

Alexus took Kitty's hands in hers and then dropped them, smiling with wide green eyes that had seemed cold earlier but were now as warm as two ripe limes hanging out in a sundrenched orchard. She turned to Bulletface and said, "Come on, girl, help me strip this nigga. And Blake, I hope you know you owe me for this."

Kitty's grin could have been pasted on with super glue, it was so stuck on her face. Her eyes maintained the same elated mien as she lifted the left side of Bulletface's dark red Givenchy hoodie and the shirt he wore underneath it. Alexus pushed up the other side, and Blake tucked his diamond chains, so they'd stay clasped around his neck as his hoodie and shirt were stripped from his dark muscular torso. Kitty remembered seeing on *E! News* that Bulletface had started working out with The Rock's personal trainer, and now she ran the palm of her hand down the rock-solid boulders and bricks of muscle that defined his chest and abdomen, she saw that those intense training sessions had paid off handsomely.

The butt of a Glock pistol protruded from behind his red croc-skin Givenchy belt. Alexus took the gun and slipped it under a pillow at the head of the bed, while Kitty, feeling more empowered with every passing second, undid Blake's belt, opened his gifted jeans, and pressed her lips against the nearly hairless portion of skin between his navel and the clean white waistband of his boxer briefs, which had *SKIMS* imprinted on it in bold, squiggly black lettering.

Kitty was peeling the jeans down his hard black thighs – and gawking at the girthy bulge in the crotch of his creamed-colored underwear – when Alexus returned and led her husband over to the bed. He kicked off his all-red Jordans and pedalled out of his jeans. Alexus shoved him violently onto the burgundy Versace comforter, biting down on her bottom lip as she did it. The expression on her face, the smirk at the corner of her mouth, was ecstatic. It elicited a small giggle from Kitty Jae and a diamond-toothed half of a grin from the gorgeous man who was arguably the greatest rapper alive.

After helping Alexus out of her snow white Balenciaga catsuit, Kitty Jae stripped down to her black lace bra and thong panties. Queen A's bra was also made of lace only it was white, and she wasn't wearing panties.

"I'll be in my bedroom down the hall," Prinny said, taking her beau by the hand and heading for the door.

"You don't need to leave," Alexus said. She and Kitty Jae were climbing on the bed.

Prinny was five feet from the door when she stopped to look back. The passionate kiss she'd shared with her man had erected an Indian tepee at the front of his pants. Her eyes flicked three places in the span of two seconds, form the Haitian's impressive bulge to his ravenous gray eyes and finally to Alexus's questioning green ones.

"No disrespect," Prinny said, "but I don't wanna see your man naked. You're like a sister to me, and he's like the big brother I didn't get to have."

Alexus sucked a tooth and sighed. "Well we need condoms. Extra-large condoms. Magnums."

Kitty Jae had condoms in her purse, but they were the regular-sized Trojans she used with Willie Mosely, the rich side nigga who'd paid for the Diamond watch Shit Breath and Rock had taken off with.

"Here, I got a couple in my wallet," said the Haitian.

Kitty couldn't remember his name, as she wasn't tryin' to. She heard his footfalls as he walked over and handed the condoms to Alexus, but she had already focused her other four senses on Bulletface. She watched his powerful chest as it rose and fell in sync with the respiratory rhythm of his full-lunged inhalations and nasal exhalations. She lowered her head to kiss and lick on the hard block of abdominal muscle that had a circular scar in the upper left corner, one of the many old bullet wounds that decorated the rap star's body like ornaments on a Christmas tree. She ran her nose over the hardening length of flesh and muscle in his boxer briefs, wanting to taste it. She heard the door swing open and click shut but again she was hardly even listening, because at that moment Alexus was curling her fingertips into the waistband of Blake's underwear and pulling them down.

Black and hard and maybe twelve inches in length, his dick came out of his boxer-briefs like a fat steel pole with a helmet on top. Kitty Jae sat back on her calves and laced her fingers under her chin, as if she were praying her thanks to God.

"Big, ain't it?" Alexus said, pumping her husband's dick in her fist. "I could hardly fit it in my mouth when we first got together, but now, when I lay on my back with my head hanging over the side of the bed, I can actually fit the whole thing in my throat."

Kitty Jae had no words, but she did have actions. So much saliva had accumulated under her tongue that some of it spilled out over her bottom lip as she moved forward, closed her hand around the base of Blake's dick, and sucked his head into her warm, wet mouth.

"This my kinda Valentine's Day right here," Blake said. He raised his hand and smacked the masked killer on Kitty Jae's left butt cheek. "Hell yeah. On the five, I'm with this. Thanks, baby."

"You can thank me with that tongue," Alexus said as she crawled up his chest and planted her plump vaginal lips right on top of his gleaming diamond grin.

With Alexus out of the way, Kitty Jae got to work, slurping Blake's huge erection in and out of her mouth, forcing it to the back of her throat and keeping it there even as she gagged and choked. She caressed his heavy ballsack with her fingers as she sucked him, feeling his testicles move around in the sack.

After a while Blake said, "*Damn*, baby, she got some *fire* ass head. You gotta start doin' that, rubbing my balls. That shit feels so good."

"Shut up," Alexus said, panting. "Just keep .. keep eatin' my pussy.. Yeah. Just like that." She was doing a jittery little bounce on his face. Her ass was just as fat and round as Nishelle's and jiggled spasmodically as she rode his tongue.

"I'm actually having a threesome with two billionaires, Kitty Jae thought. *And one of the is Bulletface.*

She smiled around the dick in her mouth and kept sucking.

The distant sound of rap music playing in the living room at the opposite end of the hallway was so faint it was unintelligible, but Kitty could tell from the beat that it was Gucci Mane and Chief Keef's "Darker".

Kitty Jae gobbled Blake's dick and massaged his balls until Alexus had an orgasm on his mouth. When Alexus recovered, Blake got to his knees and rolled one of the condoms onto the saliva-coated length of his magic stick. Kitty took off her panties and got on top of Alexus in a sixty-nine position. Her pussy was already wetter than her mouth had been, so Blake had no problem sliding right in.

"*Friday the 13th*, huh?" Blake said, and gave Jason Voorheez another smack to the hockey mask. "I'll show you a killer."

He took hold of her hips and stared fucking her senseless. There was no slow buildup, nor was there a fast build up. It was maximum speed from the very beginning. Deep, bed-rocking thrusts that took all the breath from her lungs. She'd never had a dick in her that was as thick and long as Blake's. Her baby daddy's dick was about nine inches long, but he didn't have much girth. Her current boyfriend had a good eight inches with a pretty decent girth, but Blake had him beat by a mile. Two Ton was a lovemaker, a slow stroker, a man whose sexual side only seemed to come out when there was some soft. R&B song playing in the background.

Bulletface fucked like a gangsta. He fucked like he had something to prove, like Kitty's kitten had offended him in some way and he had resolved to beat it into submission.

"Got all these make-believe killers tatted on you," he said, and yet another shark smack went across Kitty's left ass cheek. "I'm the real thing. On the Five. They need to make a scary movie about me."

His thumb slid into her butthole. She balled a handful of the comforter in one hand and gripped Alexus's meaty thigh in the other, her sharp black fingernails digging into the soft golden flesh.

"Girl, your pussy is dripping all on my chin, my neck," Alexus said, sounding amused.

Kitty Jae offered no reply. She *couldn't* reply, not even if it were possible to type the sentience out in her mind and hit the mental equivalent of the *Enter* key. For all intents and purposes, she was paralyzed from the scalp down. Her jaw hung low, like one of those terrifying little Asian characters from *The Grudge.* Her wobbling ass clapped against Balke's rapidly thrusting body again and again, smack-smack-smack-smack-smack, and then he grabbed her by the hair and yanked her head back.

"Remember that Jeezy song, "Tear it Up"? Hm? You remember that?" Bulletface asked. He waited a couple of seconds and then said, "That's the kinda time I'm on. Better ask my wife. On gang. I"ma tear dat pussy up e'ry time.. E'ry time."

This time when he slapped hero the ass she had a vision of 4K clarity: Jason peeling away from her left buttock and plunging the blood smeared blade of his butcher knife right through Blake's gut. *Teach you to slap me*, Jason would think.

Kitty Jae might have laughed at the vision if Bulletface weren't so busy plunging his giant dick into *her* guts.

Two minutes later she experienced her first ever orgasm from vaginal penetration alone. She wailed out a raging soprano of a cry and came so hard her neck cracked.

"Told you," Blake said finally— and very suddenly— stopping and pulling out of her. "Didn't I tell you? You gon' remember this dick. You gon' be ninety years old tellin' bitches at the retirement home about this dick."

He shoved Kitty Jae aside, removed his condom and tossed it onto Kitty's trembling thigh as Alexus took her place in front of him.

"He does me like that all the time," Alexus said. Frothy dollops of pussy cream spotted her face and neck. "He know he got you when he got his dick in you. A bitch cain't even talk shit. Just gotta take it."

Blake's dick was like a glorious ebony statue sticking out in front of him. "Shut up," he said, smacking his wife on the ass and watching the fat undulate like waves in the ocean. "'Cause you up next, nigga. Fuck you thought this was?"

As he guided his midnight missile into Alexus from behind, she smiled at Kitty Jae and said, "Girl, pray for me."

Kitty Joe laughed, but she also prayed.

Epilogue

A Frozen Lake

"So what's all this about?" Millionaire Markio asked.

"It's about your safety. Yours and mine too."

"And what is that supposed to mean?"

A tiny sparkle of a grin changed the shape of Alexus Costilla's face, and then it was gone. She looked flustered. Ensconced in her white fur coat, she could have been the wife of a wealthy Russian oligarch. The fat white diamonds that dangled from her ears and twinkled around her wrists and fingers refracted the midday sunlight that spilled into the white leather cabin of her sixteen passenger Bell helicopter, which her two pilots were steering east over the rippling blue waters of Lake Michigan.

Every seat on the hopper was taken. Bojo and thirteen of his stern-eyed minions occupied the remaining seats. They all had AR pistols strapped around their shoulders. The helicopter had landed on the manicured lawn behind the House of Lords, Markio's thirty million dollar Lincoln Park mansion, less than thirty minutes ago, and eight minutes later it was back in the air.

"Get on Google," Alexus said. She spoke loudly enough to be heard over the incessant churning of the rotor blades. "Look up 'The Versace Mansion,' or "Mami Beach news'. As a matter of fact, you can probably just look at any news site or news app you have on your phone."

"Just tell me what happened."

Alexus deflated in her seat. She aged five years on that defeated exhale. "Herbert Harris," she said. "He, uhh,, he somehow managed to escape, and he took Whitney Clarrett with him. Killed nine of my men. I told them not to underestimate him on account of his age. Somehow he got his hands on an ink pen, A simple fucking ink pen. That's all it took to give him the upper hand on the two armed guards who were taking him to the shower. He stabbed the first guard in both eyes and then jammed the pen up the other guy's nose, right into his brain. He used their guns to pick off the other seven guards, freed Whitney from her room, and the two of them escaped. All this happened last night, while you were out searching for Tramell and I was… Well, never mind what I was doing. Bottom line is, Herb is free. He could be halfway to Chicago by now. Hell, he might be closer than that."

Markio knew exactly what Alexus had been doing last night. He'd heard it from Jaresha when he called her a few hours ago, to tell her that it was her sister Shalonda who'd sent the boys to rob her behind The visionary Lounge. Gucci Ball had figured it out when he was contacted by someone looking to sell a diamond Audemars wristwatch for cheap. The plan had been to catch Jaresha and Tammy together and rob only Jaresha, so that she'd think Tammy had set her up. Shalonda's motive was unclear, and Markio hadn't wasted any time thinking it over. He'd promised to get Jaresha her watch back: Gucci Ball had done just that. Sure, he'd had to shoot GoGo, the boy with the stinky breath, once in the leg to get the watch back without payment, but that was a part of the game.

"I thought you told me Herb was dead."

Alexus stuck out her bottom lip. "I never said that. What I told you was the same thing I told Princess. I told you he was gone, that he would no longer be a problem for you. I didn't exactly lie. No one could've expected a man who's eighty-two years old to murder nine men and escape. Kinda reminds me of Sylvester Stallone. *The King of Tulsa*. You ever see that show?"

"Why even keep him alive?"

"The man was the best sniper the American military has ever sent into enemy territory. Two hundred and nineteen confirmed kills. I figured I could get one last shot out of him. Maybe take out Trump. I don't know."

Shrugging one shoulder, she began examining her fingernails, Markio gritted his teeth. His two iPhones were still powered off from when he'd shut them down to charge. He took them out of his Lous Vuitton duffle bag and turned them on, half-expecting a bunch of text messages and voicemails about his ex Whitney Clarrett's sudden reappearance.

The messages exceeded his expectations.

Most of them were news links. CNN's top story was *Massacre in Miami Beach; Nine Killed, IKiss Kosmetics CEO found Alive, Blames Kidnapping on Millionaire Markio*. There was video of an emaciated Whitney Clarrett standing outside The Versace Mansion with microphones from every major news network angled toward her pale, gaunt yellow face. She spoke at the cameras with tears streaming down her hollow cheeks.

Markio didn't raise the volume to hear what she had to say.

"We were able to track down Tramell and Sadé," Alexus said, studying a cuticle. "Some drunk driver in a semi-truck T-boned their car on the Dan Ryan Expressway, right after some other chick who was texting while driving accidentally bumped the tail of their car and knocked it sideways. Both of them died."

"Drunk driver, huh?"

Alexus smiled.

"Where are you taking me?" Markio asked.

"To Michigan City, Indiana." Her green eyes glowed with joy. "Oh man. My husband and I, we had so much fun in that town. Anyway, I own a house there. It's all glass and tempered steel, ten thousand square feet of living space. Indoor pool. Excellent heating and it's right on the beach, a lakefront property with a dock and three different boats you can use."

"It's a frozen lake," Markio said.

"That it is. And you know what? I'd like to see Herb take a shot at you from a boat that's rocking back and forth in the ice cold waves of Lake Michigan. Let's see him do that."

Markio Earl had nothing more to say. He shook his head and replied to a text message on his prepaid iPhone. Yogi and CJ, two Gangster Disciples from South Bend, had sold the fifty pounds of exotic bud he'd fronted them five weeks ago. He sent a thumbs up and five pine tree emojis, implying that another fifty pounds would be enroute shortly, after he got the $175,000 they owed him.

Paco Santana, a Four Corner Hustler from off Lexington and Pulaski on Chicago's west side, had texted asking for a "30 and a 3," which meant he needed thirty more pounds of Black Cherry Gelato and three more kilos of heroin.

Millionaire Markio was a New York Times bestselling novelist and an Oscar-nominated screen writer, but he was still a high-ranking gang member, tied to the streets like the Jordans on his feet.

He was about to reply to Paco when his business phone rang with a call from a blocked number. A part of him knew who it was, but he answered anyway.

"Long time no see, nephew." The old man's voice was raspier than ever, but it was also rich and commanding, a voice that could pastor a megachurch. "Didn't think I'd remember your phone number, didja?" He laughed. Keck-keck-keck-keck-keck-.

"You might be married to my auntie." Markio said, staring at Alexus but talking to Herb, "but you ain't my uncle."

"Yeah, yeah, yeah tomato, tomahto. Just know this, Know *this*. Old Uncle Herb's comin' to getcha, Markio. Sleep tight."

Call Ended.

To Be Continued

Lock Down Publications and Ca$h Presents
Assisted Publishing Packages

Due to an increase in the price of services we have increased our prices. The prices below reflect the price increase as of 11/1/24.

BASIC PACKAGE	UPGRADED PACKAGE
$699	**$1000**
Editing	Typing
Cover Design	Editing
Formatting	Cover Design
	Formatting
	Upload eBooks to Amazon
	Upload Paperback to Amazon
ADVANCE PACKAGE	**LDP SUPREME PACKAGE**
$1,400	**$1,700**
Typing	Typing
Editing (line editing/content)	Editing (line editing/content)
Cover Design	Cover Design
Formatting	Formatting
Copyright Registration	Copyright Registration
Proofreading	Proofreading
Upload eBooks to Amazon	Set up Amazon Account
Upload Paperback to Amazon	Upload eBooks to Amazon
	Upload Paperback to Amazon
	Advertise on LDP's Amazon and Facebook Page

***

Other services available upon request.
Additional charges may apply

Lock Down Publications
P.O. Box 944
Stockbridge, GA 30281-9998
Phone: 470 303-9761
Email: lockdownpublications@gmail.com

Submission Guideline

Submit the first three chapters of your completed manuscript to ldpsubmissions@gmail.com. In the subject line add **Your Book's Title**. The manuscript must be in a Word Doc file and sent as an attachment. Document should be in Times New Roman, double spaced, and in size 12 font. Also, provide your synopsis and full contact information. If sending multiple submissions, they must each be in a separate email.

Have a story but no way to send it electronically? You can still submit to LDP/Ca$h Presents. Send in the first three chapters, written or typed, of your completed manuscript to:

LDP: Submissions Dept
P.O. Box 944
Stockbridge, GA 30281-9998

DO NOT send original manuscript. Must be a duplicate. Provide your synopsis and a cover letter containing your full contact information.

Thanks for considering LDP and Ca$h Presents.

NEW RELEASES

BLOODLINE OF A SAVAGE 1-3
THESE VICIOUS STREETS 1-3
RELENTLESS GOON 1-3
BY PRINCE A. TAUHID

THE BUTTERFLY MAFIA 1-3
BY FUMIYA PAYNE

A THUG'S STREET PRINCESS 1&2
BY MEESHA

CITY OF SMOKE 3
BY MOLOTTI

GET IT IN SLUGS 1 &2
BY B. STALL

STANDING ON HER BUSINESS 1&2
BY DG SANTANA

STEPPERS 1,2&3
THE REAL BADDIES OF CHI-RAQ
BY KING RIO

THE LANE 1&2
BY KEN-KEN SPENCE

THUG OF SPADES 1&2
LOVE IN THE TRENCHES 2
CORNER BOYS
BY COREY ROBINSON

TIL DEATH 3
BY ARYANNA

THE BIRTH OF A GANGSTER 4
BY DELMONT PLAYER

PRODUCT OF THE STREETS 1-3
BY DEMOND "MONEY" ANDERSON

NO TIME FOR ERROR
BY KEESE

MONEY HUNGRY DEMONS 1-2
BY TRANAY ADAMS

HUB CITY MENACE 1-3
BY J. WHITE

A THUGGISH PASSION 1&2
LAND OF DA HOOLIGANZ 1-4
KILLAZ ON STANDBY 1&2
BY IRA B.

FO'EVA ROLLIN 1&2
BY ASSA RAYMOND BAKER

THE LEVEL UP 1&3
BY LUXURY KING

Coming Soon from Lock Down Publications/Ca$h Presents

IF YOU CROSS ME ONCE 6
ANGEL V
By Anthony Fields

A THUGS STREET PRINCESS 3
By Meesha

CORNER BOYS 2
By Corey Robinson

THA TAKEOVER
By Keith Chandler

BETRAYAL OF A G 2
By Ray Vinci

SAVAGE FAMILY EMPIRE 1&2
SOULLESS GOON 1,2&3
THE DIRTY SIDE OF MONEY 1,2&3
By Prince

FOR MY ENEMY'S SAKE
AMBITIONS OF A SLIDER
FRESH OFF DA PORCH
By IRA B.

BY THE TRUCKLOAD 1-4
TIPPIN' THE SCALES 1-3
BAD BITCHES WIT GUNZ 3
PROBLEM SOLVED 2
By Christopher "Diesel" Hornezes

Available Now

RESTRAINING ORDER 1 & 2
By **CA$H & Coffee**

LOVE KNOWS NO BOUNDARIES 1-3
By **Coffee**

RAISED AS A GOON I, II, III & IV
BRED BY THE SLUMS I, II, III
BLAST FOR ME I & II
ROTTEN TO THE CORE I II III
A BRONX TALE I, II, III
DUFFLE BAG CARTEL I II III IV V VI
HEARTLESS GOON I II III IV V
A SAVAGE DOPEBOY I II
DRUG LORDS I II III
CUTTHROAT MAFIA I II
KING OF THE TRENCHES
By **Ghost**

LAY IT DOWN I & II
LAST OF A DYING BREED I II
BLOOD STAINS OF A SHOTTA I & II III
By **Jamaica**

LOYAL TO THE GAME I II III
LIFE OF SIN I, II III
By **TJ & Jelissa**

IF LOVING HIM IS WRONG…I & II
LOVE ME EVEN WHEN IT HURTS I II III
By **Jelissa**

PUSH IT TO THE LIMIT
By **Bre' Hayes**

BLOODY COMMAS I & II
SKI MASK CARTEL I, II & III
KING OF NEW YORK I II, III IV V
RISE TO POWER I II III
COKE KINGS I II III IV V
BORN HEARTLESS I II III IV
KING OF THE TRAP I II
By **T.J. Edwards**

WHEN THE STREETS CLAP BACK I & II III
THE HEART OF A SAVAGE I II III IV
MONEY MAFIA I II
LOYAL TO THE SOIL I II III
By **Jibril Williams**

A DISTINGUISHED THUG STOLE MY HEART I II & III
LOVE SHOULDN'T HURT I II III IV
RENEGADE BOYS 1-4
PAID IN KARMA 1-3
SAVAGE STORMS 1-3
AN UNFORESEEN LOVE 1-3
BABY, I'M WINTERTIME COLD 1-3
A THUG'S STREET PRINCESS 1&2
By **Meesha**

A GANGSTER'S CODE 1-3
A GANGSTER'S SYN 1-3
THE SAVAGE LIFE 1-3
CHAINED TO THE STREETS 1-3
BLOOD ON THE MONEY 1-3
A GANGSTA'S PAIN 1-3
BEAUTIFUL LIES AND UGLY TRUTHS
CHURCH IN THESE STREETS
By **J-Blunt**

CUM FOR ME 1-8
An LDP Erotica Collaboration

BLOOD OF A BOSS 1-5
SHADOWS OF THE GAME
TRAP BASTARD
By **Askari**

THE STREETS BLEED MURDER 1-3
THE HEART OF A GANGSTA 1-3
By **Jerry Jackson**

WHEN A GOOD GIRL GOES BAD
By **Adrienne**

THE COST OF LOYALTY 1-3
By **Kweli**

BRIDE OF A HUSTLA 1-3
THE FETTI GIRLS 1-3
CORRUPTED BY A GANGSTA 1-4
BLINDED BY HIS LOVE
THE PRICE YOU PAY FOR LOVE 1-3
DOPE GIRL MAGIC 1-3
By **Destiny Skai**

A KINGPIN'S AMBITION
A KINGPIN'S AMBITION II
I MURDER FOR THE DOUGH
By **Ambitious**

TRUE SAVAGE 1-7
DOPE BOY MAGIC 1-3
MIDNIGHT CARTEL 1-3
CITY OF KINGZ 1&2
NIGHTMARE ON SILENT AVE
THE PLUG OF LIL MEXICO 1&2
CLASSIC CITY
By **Chris Green**

A GANGSTER'S REVENGE 1-4
THE BOSS MAN'S DAUGHTERS 1-5
A SAVAGE LOVE 1&2
BAE BELONGS TO ME 1&2
A HUSTLER'S DECEIT 1-3
WHAT BAD BITCHES DO 1-3
SOUL OF A MONSTER 1-3
KILL ZONE
A DOPE BOY'S QUEEN 1-3
TIL DEATH 1-3
IMMA DIE BOUT MINE 1-6
DYING FOR LIKES
By **Aryanna**

A DOPEBOY'S PRAYER
By **Eddie "Wolf" Lee**

THE KING CARTEL 1-3
By **Frank Gresham**

THESE NIGGAS AIN'T LOYAL 1-3
By **Nikki Tee**

GANGSTA SHYT 1-3
By **CATO**

THE ULTIMATE BETRAYAL
By **Phoenix**

BOSS'N UP 1-3
By **Royal Nicole**

I LOVE YOU TO DEATH
By **Destiny J**

I RIDE FOR MY HITTA
I STILL RIDE FOR MY HITTA
By **Misty Holt**

LOVE & CHASIN' PAPER
By **Qay Crockett**

TO DIE IN VAIN
SINS OF A HUSTLA
By **ASAD**

BROOKLYN HUSTLAZ
By **Boogsy Morina**

BROOKLYN ON LOCK 1 & 2
By **Sonovia**

GANGSTA CITY
By **Teddy Duke**

A DRUG KING AND HIS DIAMOND 1-3
A DOPEMAN'S RICHES
HER MAN, MINE'S TOO 1&2
CASH MONEY HO'S
THE WIFEY I USED TO BE 1&2
PRETTY GIRLS DO NASTY THINGS
By **Nicole Goosby**

LIPSTICK KILLAH 1-3
CRIME OF PASSION 1-3
FRIEND OR FOE 1-3
By **Mimi**

TRAPHOUSE KING 1-3
KINGPIN KILLAZ 1-3
STREET KINGS 1&2
PAID IN BLOOD 1&2
CARTEL KILLAZ 1-3
DOPE GODS 1&2
By **Hood Rich**

THE STREETS ARE CALLING
By **Duquie Wilson**

STEADY MOBBN' 1-3
THE STREETS STAINED MY SOUL 1-3
By **Marcellus Allen**

WHO SHOT YA 1-3
SON OF A DOPE FIEND 1-4
HEAVEN GOT A GHETTO 1&2
SKI MASK MONEY 1&2
By **Renta**

GORILLAZ IN THE BAY 1-4
TEARS OF A GANGSTA 1/&2
3X KRAZY 1&2
STRAIGHT BEAST MODE 1&2
By **DE'KARI**

TRIGGADALE 1-3
MURDA WAS THE CASE 1-3
By **Elijah R. Freeman**

SLAUGHTER GANG 1-3
RUTHLESS HEART 1-3
By **Willie Slaughter**

GOD BLESS THE TRAPPERS 1-3
THESE SCANDALOUS STREETS 1-3
FEAR MY GANGSTA 1-5
THESE STREETS DON'T LOVE NOBODY 1-2
BURY ME A G 1-5
A GANGSTA'S EMPIRE 1-4
THE DOPEMAN'S BODYGAURD 1&2
THE REALEST KILLAZ 1-3
THE LAST OF THE OGS 1-3
By **Tranay Adams**

MARRIED TO A BOSS 1-3
By **Destiny Skai & Chris Green**

KINGZ OF THE GAME 1-7
CRIME BOSS 1-4
By **Playa Ray**

FUK SHYT
By **Blakk Diamond**

DON'T F#CK WITH MY HEART 1&2
By **Linnea**

ADDICTED TO THE DRAMA 1-3
IN THE ARM OF HIS BOSS
By **Jamila**

LOYALTY AIN'T PROMISED 1&2
By **Keith Williams**

YAYO 1-4
A SHOOTER'S AMBITION 1&2
BRED IN THE GAME
By **S. Allen**

TRAP GOD 1-3
RICH $AVAGE 1-3
MONEY IN THE GRAVE 1-3
CARTEL MONEY 1&2
By **Martell Troublesome Bolden**

FOREVER GANGSTA 1&2
GLOCKS ON SATIN SHEETS 1&2
By **Adrian Dulan**

TOE TAGZ 1-4
LEVELS TO THIS SHYT 1&2
IT'S JUST ME AND YOU
By **Ah'Million**

KINGPIN DREAMS 1-3
RAN OFF ON DA PLUG
By **Paper Boi Rari**

THE STREETS MADE ME 1-3
By **Larry D. Wright**

CONFESSIONS OF A GANGSTA 1-4
CONFESSIONS OF A JACKBOY 1-3
CONFESSIONS OF A HITMAN
CONFESSIONS OF A DOPE BOY
By **Nicholas Lock**

I'M NOTHING WITHOUT HIS LOVE
SINS OF A THUG
TO THE THUG I LOVED BEFORE
A GANGSTA SAVED XMAS
IN A HUSTLER I TRUST
By **Monet Dragun**

QUIET MONEY 1-3
THUG LIFE 1-3
EXTENDED CLIP 1&2
A GANGSTA'S PARADISE
By **Trai'Quan**

CAUGHT UP IN THE LIFE 1-3
THE STREETS NEVER LET GO 1-3
By **Robert Baptiste**

NEW TO THE GAME 1-3
MONEY, MURDER & MEMORIES 1-3
By **Malik D. Rice**

CREAM 2-3
THE STREETS WILL TALK
By **Yolanda Moore**

THE STREETS WILL NEVER CLOSE 1-3
By **K'ajji**

LIFE OF A SAVAGE 1-4
A GANGSTA'S QUR'AN 1-4
MURDA SEASON 1-3
GANGLAND CARTEL 1-3
CHI'RAQ GANGSTAS 1-4
KILLERS ON ELM STREET 1-3
JACK BOYZ N DA BRONX 1-3
A DOPEBOY'S DREAM 1-3
JACK BOYS VS DOPE BOYS 1-3
COKE GIRLZ
COKE BOYS
SOSA GANG 1&2
BRONX SAVAGES
BODYMORE KINGPINS
BLOOD OF A GOON
By **Romell Tukes**

CONCRETE KILLA 1-3
VICIOUS LOYALTY 1-3
BLOODY MONEY BAGS
By **Kingpen**

THE ULTIMATE SACRIFICE 1-6
KHADIFI
IF YOU CROSS ME ONCE 1-3
ANGEL 1-4
IN THE BLINK OF AN EYE
By **Anthony Fields**

THE LIFE OF A HOOD STAR
By **Ca$h & Rashia Wilson**

NIGHTMARES OF A HUSTLA 1-3
BLOOD AND GAMES 1&2
By **King Dream**

GHOST MOB
By **Stilloan Robinson**

HARD AND RUTHLESS 1&2
MOB TOWN 251
THE BILLIONAIRE BENTLEYS 1-3
REAL G'S MOVE IN SILENCE
By **Von Diesel**

MOB TIES 1-7
SOUL OF A HUSTLER, HEART OF A KILLER 1-3
GORILLAZ IN THE TRENCHES
OOPS CRY TOO 1&2
THE DAUGHTER OF A CARTEL BOSS
By **SayNoMore**

BODYMORE MURDERLAND 1-3
THE BIRTH OF A GANGSTER 1-4
By **Delmont Player**

FOR THE LOVE OF A BOSS 1&2
By **C. D. Blue**

KILLA KOUNTY 1-5
TENDER
By **Khufu**

MOBBED UP 1-4
THE BRICK MAN 1-5
THE COCAINE PRINCESS 1-10
STEPPERS 1-3
SUPER GREMLIN 1-4
A GANGSTA'S SON
By **King Rio**

MONEY GAME 1&2
By **Smoove Dolla**

A GANGSTA'S KARMA 1-5
By **FLAME**

KING OF THE TRENCHES 1-3
By **GHOST & TRANAY ADAMS**

BAD BITCHES WIT GUNZ 1&2
PROBLEM SOLVED
By **"Christopher Diesel" Hornezes**

QUEEN OF THE ZOO 1&2
By **Black Migo**

GRIMEY WAYS 1-3
BETRAYAL OF A G
By **Ray Vinci**

XMAS WITH AN ATL SHOOTER
By **Ca$h & Destiny Skai**

KING KILLA 1&2
By **Vincent "Vitto" Holloway**

BETRAYAL OF A THUG 1&2
By **Fre$h**

COUNTDOWN OF A KILLA 1&2
SEX, MURDER AND GOD 1&2
GUNS DOWN, BOTTOMS UP 1&2
By **Lo-Life**

THE MURDER QUEENS 1-7
By **Michael Gallon**

FOR THE LOVE OF BLOOD 1-4
By **Jamel Mitchell**

THE REAL BADDIES OF CHI-RAQ 3 | KING RIO

HOOD CONSIGLIERE 1&2
NO TIME FOR ERROR
By **Keese**

PROTÉGÉ OF A LEGEND 1,2&3
LOVE IN THE TRENCHES 1&2
By **Corey Robinson**

THE PLUG'S RUTHLESS DAUGHTER 1&2
By **Tony Daniels**

BORN IN THE GRAVE 1-3
CRIME PAYS
By **Self Made Tay**

MOAN IN MY MOUTH
By **XTASY**

TORN BETWEEN A GANGSTER AND A GENTLEMAN
By **J-BLUNT & Miss Kim**

LOYALTY IS EVERYTHING 1-3
CITY OF SMOKE 1-3
By **Molotti**

HERE TODAY GONE TOMORROW 1&2
By **Fly Rock**

WOMEN LIE MEN LIE 1-4
FIFTY SHADES OF SNOW 1-3
STACK BEFORE YOU SPLURGE
GIRLS FALL LIKE DOMINOES
NAÏVE TO THE STREETS
By **ROY MILLIGAN**

PILLOW PRINCESS
By **S. Hawkins**

THE REAL BADDIES OF CHI-RAQ 3 | KING RIO

THE BUTTERFLY MAFIA 1-3
SALUTE MY SAVAGERY 1&2
By **Fumiya Payne**

THE LANE 1&2
By Ken-Ken Spence

THE PUSSY TRAP 1-5
By **Nene Capri**

DIRTY DNA
By **Blaque**

SANCTIFIED AND HORNY
by **XTASY**

BOOKS BY LDP'S CEO, CA$H

TRUST IN NO MAN
TRUST IN NO MAN 2
TRUST IN NO MAN 3
BONDED BY BLOOD
SHORTY GOT A THUG
THUGS CRY
THUGS CRY 2
THUGS CRY 3
TRUST NO BITCH
TRUST NO BITCH 2
TRUST NO BITCH 3
TIL MY CASKET DROPS
RESTRAINING ORDER
RESTRAINING ORDER 2
IN LOVE WITH A CONVICT
LIFE OF A HOOD STAR
XMAS WITH AN ATL SHOOTER